Criminal Kind

A Charlie McClung Mystery

By Mary Anne Edwards

Publisher: CreateSpace Independent Publishing Platform

ISBN-13: 9781512289978

ISBN-10: 1512289973

Cover Design – Michael James Canales

www.MaryAnneEdwards.com

To my husband, Jeff, for being practically perfect.

I want to give a special thank you to Gina, my forever best friend, for her unending friendship and superb medical knowledge. Also, thank you to Melissa for her pathology and forensic wisdom, to Doctor David Ciambrone for his vast knowledge of poisons, to Mary Kirkman for her incredible food allergen knowledge, to Terry Falletich, my personal cruise consultant, to my father-in-law, retired Chief Mike Edwards, and to my parents, Mingo & Peggy Gonzales for their prayers. A very special thank you to my beta readers, Sarah Bird and Rick Caruso. Gretchen Smith, you have my deepest gratitude. I can't forget my Street Team. THANK YOU!

Also by Mary Anne Edwards

Brilliant Disguise

A Good Girl

"Cause you're the criminal kind, you're the criminal kind.

Man, what you gonna do? Where you gonna hide?

They're callin' you a sickness, disease of the mind.

Man, what you gonna do? You're the criminal kind."

Tom Petty

Chapter 1

Marian felt Charlie get out of the bed. She watched him move like a cat on the hunt, soundlessly sprinting toward the cabin door. The bright moon bathed their suite with soft light, filtering through the double-wide sliding glass doors. She sat up, studying him as he stared out of the tiny peephole. Glancing at the clock, she saw the time, 2:14, glow on its face, she wondered what could be going on this early in the morning to awaken her husband, and she decided to join him.

The low rumble of the ship's engines was the only sound in their cabin as Marian tip-toed silently behind him and whispered, "Charlie, what's the matter?"

"Something strange is happening in the suite next to us," breathed Charlie.

Marian put her ear on the door, cold like a meat locker. Their noses almost touching, Charlie kissed the tip of hers as she strained to hear whatever he was listening to. Shuffling feet, muted voices, and a man's sorrowful moan.

"Let me see." Marian's hand slid across Charlie's bare back as she jockeyed for the peephole.

He put his finger to his lips then motioned toward the door handle. Marian slipped behind Charlie as he opened the door just a sliver. She ducked her head under his arm and stared at the people congregating in the hall. Two men pulled a gurney out of the suite, a sheet-covered body laid on it.

Charlie stepped out into the hallway, ignoring the fact he was shirtless, and in a hushed voice asked, "What's going on?"

Marian quickly retrieved two plush robes, perks from the cruise line for booking the owner's suite. Throwing on one of them, she hurried into the hallway after grabbing her husband's detective ID. Charlie carried it with him at all times, keeping it bedside while he slept. She thrust the other robe and the badge into Charlie's hands.

He flashed the small gold shield then tugged on the robe. One of the men pulling the gurney tilted his head toward the plush cabin and mouthed the words, *Go in*.

Marian shadowed Charlie into the suite. The ship's medical officer was standing with his back toward the bathroom as a man knelt over the toilet. The doctor recognized them from yesterday's VIP ship's tour; Marian having entertained him with dozens of questions.

"Doctor Nelson, what's happened?" Charlie asked as he glanced around the cabin, scrutinizing it for any clues for the cause of the sheet covered body. He noticed the bed had been turned down for the night and a green foil-covered rectangle of complimentary chocolate was in the center of one of the two pillows at the head of the bed. Looking in the silver trashcan next to the bed, he saw the wadded wrapper from the missing second piece. Spots of white, tinged with a hint of blue, dotted the carpet, trailing from the bathroom to the foot of the bed. Charlie looked in the bathroom again, the basin and vanity were covered with the same stains, the water was running, and things were knocked over on the vanity. The mirror was decorated with dried spots of the same color.

The ship's doctor had dressed hastily in his white uniform, buttons and buttonholes missed-matched. He shook his head with gray tufts of hair sticking up and glanced over his shoulder at the man, now sitting on the tiled floor, staring at nothing. Lightly touching the man's shoulder, he asked, "Mr. Ferguson, why don't you come and sit with us? I'll get you a drink."

The man, haggard from anguish, flinched from the single tap but followed the doctor to the small sitting room. He stood staring at a loveseat as if he didn't know what it was used for. Doctor Nelson prompted the mournful man to sit down.

Marian sat next to the silent man and held his hand. Peter Ferguson's grief was obvious, which only meant the body under the sheet was that of his wife's. She thought how cruel life could be; how a person's comfortable and happy world can suddenly crumble into a miserable mess. Marian knew there was nothing she could say that could make his pain go away. If she tried, it would only trivialize his feelings. "Mr. Ferguson," she murmured as she squeezed his hand and lightly rubbed his thick forearm. The memory of the night that Lee had died nudged her thoughts. *No, that's the past and I'm not going that way. This is not about me, it's about Mr. Ferguson.*

Peter Ferguson stared at her as tears ran down his puffy cheeks, lips trembling with unspoken words. Slowly, his head began to tilt toward Marian. She cradled his head on her shoulder as he hugged her tightly, like he did the first day of their cruise, during the reception celebrating the renewal of his wedding vows after 35 years of marriage.

Charlie squeezed the back of Marian's neck and kissed the top of her head as he set a glass of water on the oval coffee table. Marian could see the strain in his eyes. She thought, *but for the grace of God, there go I.* Marian didn't know what had happened to Peter Ferguson's wife, Tammy, but she wondered if the roles had been reversed, would Tammy console Charlie. Not that Tammy was unkind, she was very friendly but appeared to have an edge of restraint; the stiff hugs everyone received from Tammy were so unlike the gregarious hugs Peter had doled out.

Marian watched Charlie deliberately patrolling the cabin, discreetly examining its contents, while speaking with the ship's doctor. He looked inside the sweating ice bucket by lifting the lid with a tissue. *Where does he keep those tissues? His hand was empty, then poof, a tissue is in his hand.*

She read the doctor's lips, *anaphylactic shock.* Marian looked around the suite and wondered what Tammy could have been allergic to. There were three beautiful flower arrangements – two, she recognized from the Ferguson's renewal ceremony – an empty bottle of champagne, a bottle of merlot, two wine glasses, an open box of Godiva chocolates, and a bowl of trail mix sitting on the coffee table; nothing that appeared to be lethal or out of the ordinary.

Peter Ferguson loosened his grip on Marian and mumbled, "Sorry. I'm sorry … I … I need a …" he wiped his swollen bloodshot eyes with the heels of his meaty hands. Peter cleared his throat and swallowed. "Uh … a drink. I need a drink."

Marian reached for the water.

Peter stood, "No, I need something stronger." Taking a few steps, he stumbled and fell to his knees, a pair of beige satin pumps lay crushed under his legs. He sat on the floor clutching one of the shoes to his chest sobbing, "Tammy, Tammy, Tammy."

Marian felt tears rolling down her cheeks as she watched Peter cling to his wife's shoe. Looking around the spacious cabin, she saw remnants of Tammy's life; a pale blue silk nightgown lay across the foot of the bed, a pair of pantyhose and a bra dangled from the back of a padded side chair. A lipstick-stained champagne glass sat on the end table, next to it was a well-worn Jackie Collins' paperback novel, *Lovers and Gamblers*, with a pair of black cat-eye, rhinestone-studded reading glasses lying on top of the book.

Doctor Nelson knelt beside Peter. "Mr. Ferguson, why don't you come to the infirmary with me? I'll give you something to steady your nerves. We'll find you another cabin, so you can rest."

Peter Ferguson violently shook his head. He seized the other pump, clenching the pair tightly to his chest as if he could give life to them as if he could force Tammy back to life to reclaim her magical shoes.

"Very well," Doctor Nelson conceded quickly. He didn't know what he could give to the man anyway. Peter Ferguson reeked of alcohol, any drug given could be lethal. "Would you like for me to stay with you?"

Again, Peter Ferguson shook his head. He stood, dropped the shoes, sat on the edge of the bed, grabbed the nightgown, buried his face in it and then laid down holding the gown in a tender embrace. He was still, very still, as if he were dead.

With two long strides, Doctor Nelson was by the bed feeling for a pulse. The doctor's bunched-up shoulders relaxed. The grieving man had passed out, probably from drinking too much. *Just as well*, he thought, *just as well*. "I'll stay with him until the morning, then play it by ear." The doctor looked at Charlie. "I'd like to speak to you tomorrow about this. Something's…" Doctor Nelson paused and pursed his lips. Sighing, he continued, "We'll talk in the morning. You two go back to bed and enjoy your honeymoon."

Chapter 2

Marian felt Charlie's strong arms pulling her close, her back fitting perfectly against his wide chest. He kissed the back of her neck sending goose bumps cascading over her slender body.

"Good morning, Mrs. McClung." Charlie's warm breath caressed Marian's ear in a way that only a lover's can.

Snuggling in closer, Marian sighed, "Good morning, Mr. McClung." She felt his arousal and turned in his arms.

Someone rapped gently on the door then rang the doorbell. Marian's eyes popped open, bright sunlight blurred her vision as she searched for the clock. "What time is it?" She couldn't believe it was already room service with their breakfast. It wasn't supposed to be delivered until 9:30.

"It's nine thirty-three," groaned Charlie. His feet hit the floor with a heavy thud. He pulled on his robe, loosely cinching it closed, and then slid the curtain around the bed, shielding Marian from prying eyes.

"Good morning, Mr. McClung. I have breakfast for you and Madam." Henry, their butler, stood in the doorway waiting for Charlie to invite him in the cabin.

"Please, come in." Charlie led the way toward the dining table.

Henry meticulously laid the table for breakfast. Each utensil exactly a quarter inch apart. "Shall I pour out the coffee? Or perhaps, some freshly squeezed orange juice to start your morning?"

"Yes, that would be perfect, Henry," replied Charlie, his thoughts were still on what lay behind the curtain.

Henry's left eyebrow arched. "You would like to start off with orange juice while your coffee cools?"

Charlie smiled at his own blunder and Henry's finesse. "Yes, you read my mind, Henry." *I've got to leave this guy a good tip.*

With a steady hand, the butler poured the beverages. "Shall I serve breakfast?"

"No, thank you. We can do that."

Henry bowed slightly. "Very good, sir. Do you or Madam require anything? Anything at all? Perhaps, freshen up your fruit basket?"

Charlie glanced at the overflowing basket with one missing banana. "That's very kind of you, Henry, but I think this is all we need for now."

Tilting his head toward the curtain-enclosed bed, Henry addressed Marian, "Madam, I wish for you a very pleasant day."

For no reason, Marian blushed. "Thank you, Henry."

Henry then looked at Charlie and with a courteous nod said, "Sir." Turning on his heels, Henry left the cabin.

At the sound of the cabin door closing, Marian poked her head through the bed curtains. "Is the coast clear? I'm starving!"

With a wicked grin on his face, Charlie slid open the curtains. "From Henry, yes, but not from me." He picked up Marian and planted a big kiss on her mouth. "Now, where were we?"

"Oh, Charlie, you beast," laughed Marian. "Shouldn't we eat first? You know, to build up your strength after last night?"

He released his firm grip, dropping her on the bed. "You're right. Food is more appealing right now." Charlie sat at the table and dished out scrambled eggs onto their plates.

Marian gaped at her new husband. "Really?"

"You said I needed to build up my strength." With his bare foot, Charlie pushed an empty chair from the table. "Come on, eat, and build up your strength." He winked, "You're going to need it, Mrs. McClung." He scooped up a fork full of eggs, and then looked at her lying on her back, propped up on her elbows, wearing practically nothing. *God, I'm a lucky man.* He dropped his fork and growled, "Just kidding" and pounced toward Marian. On all fours, he hovered over her, staring at her beautiful body. "I think I have just enough energy to—," He then leaned down and began to kiss her neck.

"I knew you couldn't resist me," Marian purred as she pulled Charlie down on top of her.

"Mmm, why would I ever want to?"

Chapter 3

Marian reclined on a thickly padded lounger, her red one-piece bathing suit, similar to the one Christie Brinkley wore on the cover of *Time*, was a nice contrast to the blue material of the cushion. Near the ship's pool, but away from the noisy cruisers splashing in its crystal clear water, yet not too far removed for people watching, she basked in the warm sea breezes keeping her cool from the bright sunlight filtering through the pergola. She hoped Charlie would soon join her.

The view of the bar was excellent, particularly interesting because Peter Ferguson seemed to have progressed through the stages of grief fairly quickly. Maybe it was due to the pretty blonde sitting next to him at the bar, her long hair danced in the wind, coyly brushing against his face and bare shoulder like that of a mistress. *Hmm, maybe he's laughing to keep from crying*. From behind her dark Audrey Hepburn sunglasses, Marian studied the nuances of their interactions.

Someone's breath on Marian's ear caused her to gasp, choking on the Diet Dr Pepper she was sipping mindlessly as she spied on Peter Ferguson and his new friend.

"I'm sorry! I didn't mean to scare you. I thought you saw me walk up." Charlie grabbed the thick towel that Marian had been using to reserve the empty lounger next to her, his paperback, *Ham on Rye*, bounced into her lap. He began to blot the spilled soda from her chest.

"What's got you—," he looked in the direction that had her so entranced, he paused, "Well, I'll be …"

"Yeah, right? His wife's barely dead and he's flirting—,"

"Jack!" Charlie walked toward Peter Ferguson and the blonde girl, grinning and waving. The two were oblivious to Charlie, but a laughing, tall, thin man with a mass of black hair, threw up his hands happy to see him.

"McClung, well I'll be damned."

Marian watched her husband and the man he'd called Jack, shake hands, like two long-lost brothers. *Hmm, Jack, Jack. Jack! The medical examiner.*

"Jack, this is my wife, Marian. Marian meet Jack Jackson."

"So nice to meet you, Mrs. McClung." Jack shook her hand gently.

She smiled at the sound of being called *Mrs. McClung*; her heart pounded seeing the pride and love on Charlie's face as he introduced her as his wife. "Please call me, Marian. Pull up a chair, Jack … may I call you, Jack?"

The thin man slid an unoccupied lounger in front of theirs, sitting on its edge, and faced Marian and Charlie. "I'll answer to almost anything, so Jack is fine, Marian." Smiling, he glanced at Charlie, "I didn't know you were married. I don't recall seeing that silver band on your finger when we met."

Charlie reached over toward Marian, clasped her hand then kissed her knuckles. "Two weeks, we're on our honeymoon."

"Congratulations! Drinks on me, what'll you have?" Not waiting for a reply, he jumped up, looked at his watch, rubbed his hands

together and pronounced, "Champagne! It's gotta be champagne!"
Jack went to the bar, placed his order then returned. "They hav'ta go
get it, don't keep the good stuff at the pool bar, Dom Perignon, nothing
after 1970!"

Marian choked on the Diet Dr Pepper, again. "Jack, that's too
extravagant," Charlie protested as he again cleaned spilled soda from
Marian's legs.

"Hey, my pleasure. We'll toast your nuptials and my promotion.
I've gotta find happiness somewhere," Jack replied with a smile tinged
with sadness. "Yep, I booked this cruise over a month ago, after my
promotion, thanks to you, Charlie."

Charlie grinned, "You're one of the finest medical examiners I've
worked with. Don't diminish your talent. I should be buying you a
drink for helping solve the Pannell case."

Watching the two men inflate each other's egos, Marian wondered
why Jack appeared to be upset when he was apparently thrilled by his
promotion; he booked a cruise to celebrate it. Charlie must have read
her mind because he asked the question before she could form the
words.

"Are you here with your wife?"

Holding up his tanned hand, Jack wiggled his ring finger, with a
pale outline of where a ring had once been and smirked, "You know
the answer to that question already, don't you?"

"Divorce or separation?"

"Separation, but it'll end up in divorce. She said she couldn't stand
playing second fiddle to a bunch of corpses." He ran his fingers

through his hair, scratching along the way to the back of his neck. "My newly divorced sister is with me instead." Jack looked toward the bar then scanned the deck crammed with a variety of sunbathers in various stages of sunburn, some practically naked, some almost completely clothed. "She was at the bar but who knows where she's flitted off to, I guess enjoying her freedom from being shackled to a mind-numbing bore, her words not mine. I liked the guy, a brilliant computer mastermind."

A deeply-tanned waiter in navy blue shorts and a white polo shirt trimmed in the same shade of blue as his shorts sat a champagne bucket filled with ice beside Jack. "Señor Jack! Your champagne as requested." The waiter pulled the dark bottle from its nest of ice and read the label, "Dom Perignon, 1970. Ah, Señor Jack, you have mighty fine taste." The waiter beamed, "Would you like for me to open?"

"Diego, you read my mind. I'd probably put out someone's eye with the cork, more than likely, my own."

With the champagne poured, Jack held up his glass, the tapered flute already sweating in the Caribbean heat, "To McClung and Marian, may your love thrive beyond eternity."

After a few minutes of chit-chat, Charlie leaned toward Marian and kissed her temple, "Honey, do you mind if I talk shop with Jack, about last night?"

Marian smiled, "You know I love a good mystery." She held out her glass for more champagne.

"Last night? What happened?" Jack asked as he filled Marian's glass.

A pair of black Ray Bans hid Charlie's eyes, while he surveyed the mass of bodies around the pool or tucked under shady spots. *Any one of these people, including the staff, none of them looking like the criminal kind, could be hiding vile thoughts or sins. He hated the fact that years of police work had forever made him inherently suspicious of nearly everyone he met.* He finished his glass of champagne, tilting the empty toward Jack. "Mmm, this is a very good year. Thanks, but I digress." Charlie moved to sit at the foot of Marian's lounger so Jack could better hear him over the shouts from the Congo line that had just formed.

Marian sat up, leaning against Charlie's bare back, she kissed his ear and whispered, "You're not going to leave me out of this conversation."

"I wouldn't dream of it." He patted her cheek, dreaming of scooping her up, taking her back to their cabin, tossing her on the bed, and …

Jack stood, coughed, and then said, "Feeling like a third wheel, I think I'll go sit at the bar and leave you two lovebirds alone. We can talk about last night some other time."

Both blushing, Charlie and Marian insisted that Jack sit back down. "Last night, rather, early this morning, Tammy Ferguson was found dead in her cabin by her husband, Peter. They have the owner's suite next to ours."

"And you think it was foul play?"

"Yep."

Jack drained his glass, placed it upside down in the ice bucket, topped off Marian's glass with the last of the champagne, and then shoved the bottle upside-down in the melting ice. "What did the ship's doctor say about it?"

Charlie tugged his earlobe, "Well, he thinks it's anaphylactic shock but caused by what, he has no clue. I did a cursory look around the cabin last night after the body had been removed and didn't see anything obvious laying around. The husband said she was mildly allergic to peanuts and shellfish, just a few hives and itching, that's all. And according to the husband, she avoided them like the plague even though they weren't life-threatening. Said she'd scratch like a dog with fleas."

"Have you seen her body?"

Marian leaned over toward the ice bucket, her warm, bare skin brushed across Charlie's shoulders as she placed her empty glass in the ice bucket dripping with condensation. The mental image of Tammy's thick bluish lips kept his thoughts on her mysterious death. "Yeah, I was with the doctor just before I saw you." He rubbed his throat. "There were deep scratches on her throat, claw marks, and her tongue was so swollen it protruded from her puffy blue lips, and she had big welts and a bad rash around her mouth, throat, upper body, and both hands." He felt Marian shiver. He rubbed the goosebumps on her arm.

Jack scratched his temple. "Yeah, definitely sounds like anaphylactic shock. Hmm, you said the husband found her early this morning. He wasn't there when it happened?"

"Nope. Walked into the cabin and found her lying at the foot of the bed. Now, get this, they renewed their wedding vows day before yesterday. So, you'd think they'd have been celebrating together."

Marian leaned away from Charlie and gasped, "What? You're kidding! He was out all night, drinking, or whatever, while she was alone in the cabin, dying?" She stood, wrapping a sheer tropical print sarong around her narrow waist, tying it as if she were angry with it, and said, "I'm going to get to the bottom of this."

Both men stood.

Charlie placed his hands gently on her shoulders, "Honey, how are you going to get to the bottom of this?" In a matter of seconds, he witnessed her face transform from anger to mild confusion, then to sorrow. "Oh, Marian, don't cry. I didn't mean to make you cry." He wrapped his arms around her. "Let's go back to our cabin, okay? We'll talk about it."

She pulled away, smiled, and with her fingertips, wiped away the tears from the corners of her eyes. "I'm sorry. I know I'm overreacting, but to think of Tammy dying alone, struggling for breath, when her husband should have been with her, just makes me, so … so angry and sad." Plopping down on the lounger, she looked up at Charlie and then to Jack. "Please sit down, let's solve this together. Three heads have got to be better than two, right?" Marian asked with a nervous laugh. With a pleading stare at her husband, she patted the cushion beside her, and said softly, "Sweetie."

Charlie and Jack looked at one another, shrugged and sat down as directed.

"So, what's the plan?" Marian murmured, resting her chin on Charlie's shoulder.

Sighing, Charlie worried that his gentle bride may get herself in trouble again. In less than four months, he had to save her life, two times. But then again, she wasn't truly at fault either time, just pissed-off women looking for someone to pin the blame on, unfortunately, they chose Marian. "Look, it's—," Charlie's words were chopped off by his new wife's don't-you-go-there glare.

"Oh, no, Mr. Charlie McClung! You married me and you're stuck with me. We became one for better or for worse. So we are in this together." Marian saw his lip tremble and his right eye twitch. "Don't say a word until I'm finished."

He opened his mouth to protest but resigned himself to silence. *She's a stubborn beauty.*

"This is o*ur* honeymoon. And if you choose to investigate a murder on *our* honeymoon then I'm going to be right there beside you. You're not going to abandon me," her lip quivered as she thought of Tammy.

Charlie laughed. "Honey, I'll never ever abandon you." He kissed her forehead and asked, "Tell me why I *need* you in this investigation, why's that?"

"Well, first of all, I can talk to people without them suspecting me, you know, get them to open up just by being a nosy-body." She grinned, "Joan thinks I should've been a lawyer."

Charlie reached for his wife's hand, "Okay, Miss Marple, no make that Mata Hari," Charlie replied with a wink. "First of all, we don't even know if it is a murder, could be an unfortunate accident. Second,

I don't want you to go getting yourself almost killed, again. You might just accomplish it if there's a next time which wouldn't make me at all happy."

"Well, that makes me happy to hear that you'd be unhappy." Marian slid her arms around his waist and kissed him passionately.

Jack scribbled something on a cocktail napkin and waved it in the air. "OK, I give up! Here's my cabin number; you two call me when your hormones settle down. If I'm not there, you'll probably find me right over there," and he walked toward the pool bar.

Chapter 4

"Doctor Nelson, this is my friend, Doctor Jack Jackson, an associate medical examiner with the Georgia Bureau of Investigation." Charlie shook hands with the ship's doctor as he made the introductions.

Doctor Nelson grinned, "You're rather young to hold such a position; I congratulate you."

"I'm one of eight examiners actually, but thank you for the compliment, and by the way, I just look young. Darn my boyish good looks."

Doctor Nelson slapped Jack's back. "I like a doctor with a sense of humor. The only way to survive in this profession." He turned and motioned for Charlie and Jack to follow him. "Am I correct to assume McClung has informed you of my suspicion concerning the death of Tammy Ferguson?" He unlocked an oversized door, tugging to pull it open. The frigid air exploded from the small room, a solitary occupied gurney before them. Doctor Nelson passed a box of latex gloves to Jack.

Jack pulled the sheet away from Tammy's upper body. Her lips were beyond swollen, a scarlet rash dripped from her mouth and down her chin. He lightly touched a pale blue crust that seemed to have erupted from her mouth flowing down her chin, following the path of the rash, or was it the other way around? Opening her mouth gently, he peered inside. "May I use your otoscope?"

Doctor Nelson rolled an instrument stand next to the gurney.

Selecting a tongue depressor and the otoscope, Jack began to probe the inflamed tissue. "Mmm, it looks like …" he smelled her mouth, "yeah, toothpaste." He looked at the two men. "I'm going to venture to guess it was something in the toothpaste that caused this reaction." Jack studied her hands. "She must have been right-handed." He pointed to the rash running across the fingertips of the left hand. "See here and there's a substantial rash on the palm of the right one. She held the brush with her right hand and wiped off the paste as it drooled from her mouth. Like this," Jack demonstrated by air-brushing his teeth and wiping his mouth.

"Makes sense." Charlie tugged his earlobe. "But I've never heard of anyone being allergic to toothpaste."

"Hmm, it's very rare, and honestly, I've never heard of a case of someone dying from it." Jack continued with the examination. "There are a few bruises on her shoulders, probably from bouncing around the room while she struggled for breath. And the right knee is heavily bruised, I'd say from it taking all of her weight when she collapsed."

The puff of cold air vapor floated from Charlie's mouth as he grunted, "Huh. Well, I need to get into that cabin. Were you with him all night, Doctor Nelson?"

"Yes, and this morning I informed him that he would be moved to another cabin because of his wife's death, although I had not spoken to security. I knew he couldn't stay because he might destroy evidence.

I'm not totally ignorant of suspicious deaths. I was a coroner once in my younger years."

"How did he react when you told him?"

Doctor Nelson shrugged, "Well, it didn't seem to affect him in any way. Just grabbed his toiletry bag and a change of clothes and said, *lead the way.*" He laughed, "Took me by surprise. I thought he would protest like he did last night, giving me more time to speak with security and to find a suitable cabin." The doctor grinned, "I didn't know where to put him, so I took him to my cabin for a shower and a shave."

"You say he grabbed his toiletry bag? Did he put anything in it, like toothpaste?" Charlie rubbed his hands together, his breath visible as he blew on them in a vain attempt to generate some heat.

"Nope, just picked up a leather bag. It looked brand new." Doctor Nelson paused. "Well, no, that's not exactly right. He tossed in a toothbrush and comb."

Jack, oblivious to their conversation, examined Tammy's right hand, sniffed her palm and asked, "Can you smell anything?"

Doctor Nelson inhale deeply, "No."

"What?" Charlie asked with a quizzical expression.

"Just get over here and take a sniff."

Charlie obeyed. "Nope, nothing."

Jack pressed a large piece of gauze on her palm. "I think I detect a hint of garlic. Find out what she ate last night." Holding the gauze snuggly against her skin, he looked around the tiny morgue, maybe room for six bodies if positioned just right. "I'll be here for a while, why don't you two go talk to security."

Charlie was the first one out of the freezing cold room. *Never, ever will I feel comfortable in any morgue, even on a cruise ship.*

"I have to stick around the clinic for a while to see any possible patients."

And on cue, an angry woman entered, roughly guiding a man with a guilt-ridden face, holding his wrist, more than likely her husband. Doctor Nelson had treated this kind of injury before and with worse outcomes. A husband or boyfriend staring at a practically naked young thing while walking behind his wife or girlfriend, then tripping over a chaise lounge, spraining his wrist or incurring a more serious injury. These injuries frequently produced a man now totally committed to catering to his partner's every whim.

"I'll see you later." Charlie stepped around the groaning man and made his way to security.

Charlie knocked on the door of the chief of security. "May I come in?"

A bull of a man peered over half-frame reading glasses, determining if Charlie was friend or foe. He stood, extended his hand, and said, "You must be the detective Doctor Nelson mentioned this morning, Charlie McClung, right?"

"Yes, sir." The officer's grip was firm but not intimidating.

"My name is Phillip Watson. Please take a seat, Detective McClung. I understand the doc thinks we may have a suspicious death, a murder he thinks?"

Charlie took the only seat available, a navy blue, plastic cafeteria-type chair, not one for much comfort, unlike the thickly padded office chair the chief was occupying. "Thank you, please call me McClung. And yes, it appears the death of Tammy Ferguson may be murder. I'm thinking poison."

Chief Watson smiled, exposing slightly crooked teeth, one of the two front teeth somewhat overlapping the other. "My deputy said it was anaphylactic shock. Why do you think it's murder by poison?"

"Well, lucky for us, a friend of mine is onboard, a medical examiner with the Georgia Bureau of Investigation, Doctor Jack Jackson."

"Ah, how fortuitous, indeed." Chief Watson's dark brown eyes sparkled with discernment. "I guess I can safely assume, Doctor Nelson informed you of his experience as a coroner? I think he misses those days of mayhem."

Charlie liked the chief, his slight British accent reminding him of Da, and his non-territorial demeanor, unlike his old chief, Perry Miller. "Yeah, I think he does. But to get back to your first question, it appears to be anaphylactic shock. The strange thing is, it looks like she had a reaction to the toothpaste, but I'm going to guess it was the toothpaste that administered the poison."

With his index finger, Chief Watson scratched the smooth space between his nose and top lip. "Hmm, that's a new one for me, interesting theory. I'm guessing you suspect the husband?"

"Yeah, as you know, the spouse is usually the number one suspect, the same in this case, but it could've been anyone with access to their suite, the butler, concierge, room steward, even security."

The chief smiled, "Yes, even security. In other words, a shipload of suspects. Any ideas to the motive?"

Charlie shook his head. "Nope, I wanted to ask your permission to investigate or at least help with it."

The chief looked at the pile neatly stacked in his inbox and the folders laying in the middle of his desk, begging for attention. Glancing at his wristwatch, he thought for a few seconds, "My chief deputy is disembarking at the next port of call, family matters to attend, and as you can see, my desk is overflowing with paperwork. So in this case, you can have full rein to investigate. It's getting close to afternoon tea, please join me and we can sort out the details. You can invite your new wife if you'd like."

Charlie glanced toward his ring finger; he'd been turning the new wedding band unconsciously around his finger. He grinned. "You're good," and held up his left hand and wiggled his fingers. "Two weeks married, we're on our honeymoon."

Chief Phillip Watson shrugged, "Congratulations, but I don't want to intrude on your honeymoon."

"Think nothing of it. Marian, my wife, loves teatime and a good mystery. This will be perfect for her."

"She sounds delightful."

"Yep, she's that and more. Perhaps, we could have tea in our suite which is next to the Ferguson's?"

"Sounds like an excellent plan. I'll order tea and have it delivered to your suite. I'll join you in thirty minutes?"

Charlie stood and extended his hand, shaking the chief's. "It's a plan. We'll see you in a bit."

"Thank you. You've made my day. It's been awhile since I've played detective. I'm rather like Doctor Nelson. I miss it from time to time. Being on a ship can become rather monotonous with petty thieves and drunken passengers. This should prove to be a most exciting adventure."

Chapter 5

Marian was tired from doing nothing but laying around the pool, people watching. Same people coming and going, occasionally someone interesting would pass by on their way to the buffet, but neither Peter Ferguson nor the blonde ever reappeared at the poolside bar. She decided to call it a day and go to her suite and read on the veranda or maybe take a nap or better yet if she could find Charlie, maybe an afternoon of delight.

When she got to her suite, the door was wide open, she could hear a female humming. She saw a cleaning cart two cabins away from theirs. *It must be our cabin steward.* Marian entered without a second thought. A young woman was hanging towels in the bathroom. Marian remembered her name being Bella, thinking how the name suited the beautiful girl with auburn hair.

A twinge of envy pinched Marian as she noticed that Mother Nature had been most generous to the tall girl. She glanced down at her own chest. *Oh, well, it's enough, normal I guess, but she makes my chest look like a turtle's.*

Marian sighed. She found her mystery novel, *Resurrection Row*, written by her newest favorite author, Anne Perry, laying on the nightstand next to the unmade bed. Then she decided that she had had enough sun and opted for a shower instead.

Bella screamed when Marian entered the bathroom. "I'm sorry, Madam. I didn't hear you come into the cabin," Bella apologized as she pressed her hand underneath her ample bosom.

"No, it's my fault, I should have said something."

Bella backed out of the bathroom. "I'll finish later."

"No, you don't have to leave. You can finish straightening the cabin while I take a shower."

"Are you sure, Madam?"

"Yes, it's fine."

Marian locked the bathroom door. As she was undressing, she heard Bella singing, *The Great Pretender* by the Platters, and wondered how a girl so young would know a song that was released before she was born. The singing stopped abruptly. Marian heard a man's voice, Henry's voice. He sounded upset, angry. She cracked open the door and saw Bella and Henry reflected in the dresser mirror.

"Why haven't you finished in here? And stop that singing."

Bella smirked, "I was told to make up the new cabin for Mr. Ferguson, first. They moved him to a suite two decks below because his wife dropped dead last night."

"Who told you that?"

She rolled her eyes, "Our boss, who else?"

Henry took a few steps and stood almost nose-to-nose with Bella. "Does that make you happy, now that you think you have a chance at a rich man? He's old enough to be your father!"

"I say, marry them old and rich, tease them, outlive them and then cash in their life insurance. Besides …" Bella licked her thumb and then pressed it to her hip, "Tissss, hot, hot, hot! Not even you can resist this." She rubbed her body against Henry, "Remember?"

He grabbed her shoulders. "One day your teasing is going to get you in trouble."

"I always make sure the wife is nowhere in sight and this one's wife is way out of sight, as in dead."

Henry pushed her away; she fell on the partially made bed. "That's not what I mean."

Marian saw Henry's jaws tighten as he gritted his teeth. The view in the mirror was like watching a movie.

Bella giggled, "I like rough sometimes, remember?" Her green eyes seemed to sparkle. She stood, smoothing out her uniform. "You want to keep quiet, Madam is in the bathroom."

Marian shut the door quickly and as quietly as she could, praying Henry didn't see her spying when he jerked his head toward the door she hid behind. She turned on the shower hurriedly then pressed her ear against the door.

Henry must have been standing right on the other side. She heard him clearly tell Bella to hurry up and finish because he was bringing tea in less than thirty minutes and he wanted the cabin pristine and wanted her gone.

"Bella, tell the Madam that tea will be served at four o'clock and the chief of security will be joining her and her husband."

Marian heard the cabin door shut and heard Bella begin to sing the chorus of *Hurts So Good*. She gasped as Henry's words finally sunk in. "Oh, no, I've less than thirty minutes to get ready for tea."

♣

Afternoon tea was short and unspoiled. Officer Watson avoided all conversation about Tammy Ferguson's death and the impending investigation. Charlie was proud of Marian, the perfect hostess. He could see she was bursting with curiosity, a woman of a thousand questions, but she was gracious enough to let Officer Watson ramble on about the best restaurants and sights to see at each port of call.

Officer Watson left after the last drop of tea was finished, giving Marian and Charlie just enough time for a bit of afternoon delight before getting ready for the captain's dinner.

Chapter 6

Marian slid a pair of art deco diamond and sapphire dangles, a present from Charlie, into each earlobe. She started to apply ruby red lipstick then paused. "Hey, would you like a kiss before I put this on?" She waved a silver tube in the air.

"You better know it." Charlie cupped her face in his hands, kissing her tenderly but deeply.

She felt weak at the knees, wishing they weren't having dinner with the captain. "Mmm, may I have another one?"

Charlie brushed his lips on hers and then pulled back. "Can you handle another one?"

"Let's find out."

The cabin's doorbell rang, followed by a sharp knock.

"I guess we'll never find out." Charlie swatted her butt as he passed by her on his way to open the door. "Jack, come on in, Marian is decent."

Jack stopped suddenly when he saw Marian standing at the foot of the bed, looking into the full-length mirror, reapplying her lipstick. *Man, McClung's lucky,* he thought.

She turned with a brilliant smile, "Hello, Jack, so good to see you again." Marian looked him up and down. "Nice tux. You're almost as handsome as Charlie." She squeezed her husband's arm and leaned her head on his shoulder, looking up into Charlie's eyes. "No one comes close to you."

Charlie kissed the top of her head. "I'm glad love has blinded you, sweetheart."

Jack snapped his mouth closed and cleared his throat. "Charlie, I hope you don't mind me saying that your wife is stunning. Absolutely stunning!"

Holding Marian at arm's length, Charlie marveled at how beautiful she was in the sapphire blue floor-length gown, the cap sleeves accentuated her round, firm shoulders, and its neckline plunged just enough to make you wonder. "Hmm, I guess you're right. I've never noticed."

"Oh, what a charmer I married." Marian turned her attention to Jack. "Are you going to the Captain's dinner?"

"Yes, Doctor Nelson invited me to join the party."

Marian clapped her hands. "Splendid!" She held Charlie's hand and then offered her free hand to Jack. "I feel like a princess being escorted by her prince," Marian squeezed Charlie's hand, "you are my Prince Charming, darling, and Jack will be my royal knight."

They chatted about the cruise ship's luxurious carpet, the weather, and other trivial matters, not wanting to ruin the night with talk of murder, as they strolled to the captain's private dining quarters.

"Will your sister be joining us, I'd love to meet her?"

"Who knows? My sister is in her own little world, taking advantage of the eligible bachelors onboard, well at least I hope they're single." Jack sighed, "Yep, sowing her wild oats, which she said is what I should be doing instead of hanging around the dead." He scratched his head with the bottom of the champagne bottle. "She sounds like my wife, my estranged wife that is, so maybe my sister makes a good point."

Charlie cleared his throat. "I learned a long time ago, don't force your life. If it doesn't feel right, it's not right for you. That's why I waited so long for this one, the love of my life."

"Oh, Charlie, you are a charmer." Marian cooed.

"And another thing, Jack, we're not dead. After dinner, we're going dancing, we'll show you we're alive and kicking, right, Marian?"

"Yes, Jack, you must come with us, surely, as handsome as you are, you'll find someone willing to help you sow your newly found wild oats."

Jack grinned. "All right, at the very least, I'll be with the living."

♣

Charlie, Marian, and Jack were the first guests to arrive for the captain's dinner. Marian was mildly surprised to see Henry, their butler, serving before-dinner martinis. Captain Lars Halverson welcomed them, his white blonde hair was almost as white as his perfectly straight teeth. Captain Halverson introduced his first officer, Jameson Cornelia, a tall, thin man with curly auburn hair, who greeted Marian with a slight bow, Charlie and Jack received robust handshakes.

"I believe you've already met my chief of security, Officer Phillip Watson, and my medical officer, Doctor Stephen Nelson."

"Yes, sir, and I would like to introduce my wife, Marian." Charlie felt like a little boy showing off his first girlfriend, grinning like a first grader.

While Marian was speaking with the two officers, Peter Ferguson stepped through the door with a shapely blonde clinging to his forearm, the blonde that was with him at the pool bar earlier in the day. She studied Jack's expression as he caught sight of the couple and wondered if the woman was his estranged wife.

"Excuse me for a moment." Jack slipped past Charlie as he confronted the blonde.

"Jack!" The woman was a little tipsy but obviously happy to see him. She released her grip from Peter and latched on to Jack. "I'd like for you to meet an old friend of mine and co-worker, Peter Ferguson. Peter, this is my brother, Jack." She then planted a kiss on Jack's cheek leaving behind a lipstick stain.

Jack wiped the smudge from his face and whispered to his sister, "Tone it down a bit, Sophia." He extended his hand toward Peter, "Sorry for your loss." Jack grimaced as his sister pinched the soft flesh at the bend of his elbow.

Peter's salesman smile weakened for a second. "Thank you."

Sophia winked and pointed to Henry, "Peter, would you mind getting me one of those martinis?"

"Not at all, excuse me." Peter quickly retreated.

Pushing her long bleached hair behind her ears, Sophia exposed a pair of two-carat diamond studs. "What are you doing, saying a thing like that?"

"You do know that his wife died last night? How can you be acting like this, carrying on with him like nothing's happened? How can he?" Jack took a deep breath.

Sophia smiled. "Jack, don't get so upset. It's not like he killed her, besides their marriage was just a convenience." She wiggled her fingers at the first officer as he passed by.

"What's wrong with you? It's like I don't even know you." Jack rubbed his forehead, trying to force a nagging headache away. "How long have you known Peter? Is it more than a work relationship?"

She rolled her eyes. "Good god, no! There's nothing between us, just two miserable people trying to cheer each other up." Sophia saw her brother's shoulders relax. "Are we good?"

Jack pursed his lips and exhaled, "Yeah. Yeah, we're good." He looked toward Charlie, caught his attention, and then motioned him over.

"Sophia, I'd like for you to meet two of my friends, Charlie and Marian McClung, they're on their honeymoon. This is my sister, Sophia Brooks."

"Jackson, Sophia Jackson. I reclaimed my maiden name, part of the divorce agreement.

Marian daintily shook her hand. "Very nice to meet you."

"How do you know Peter Ferguson?" Charlie asked bluntly.

"What? I mean, uh, why do you ask?"

Marian choked slightly on the dirty martini she was sipping. Jack grunted at Charlie's directness.

"May I join this little party?" Peter asked as he handed Sophia a dry martini with a twist of lemon. "Mrs. McClung, thank you for comforting me last night."

"Please, call me Marian."

"Thank you, of course. I feel like were old friends after yesterday's events."

Sophia glanced at the faces, staring at her. "How do you all know each other?"

"The McClungs have the suite next to mine and attended the vow renewal ceremony. Marian was kind enough to offer her shoulder to cry on and Mr. McClung … I mean … Detective McClung, her husband, is investigating Tammy's untimely death," Peter answered with a smug grin.

"I'm a bit confused. What's to investigate? You told me she had a severe allergic reaction to something." Sophia stepped closer to her brother.

Charlie took note of Peter's word choices, his tone, and posture. "It's standard procedure. Nothing to be concerned about, Sophia."

"Dinner is served," Henry announced.

The large oval table had 16 chairs around it and 15 guests in attendance. Most of the guests seemed confused by Peter's companion and waited to choose their seats. The captain and first officer sat at each end, the chief of security and Doctor Nelson sat opposite of each other at the center of the table. Sophia quickly sat to the right of Jameson, the first officer, Peter to the left of him.

Charlie chose the seat next to Chief Phillip Watson, Marian, in between her husband and Peter. Jack was next to Doctor Nelson. The only seat vacant was between Jack and Sophia.

Captain Halverson lightly tapped a cut-crystal water glass as Henry served each guest a flute filled with Dom Perignon. "Thank you for dining with me tonight. I would like to give a toast before we dine on the sumptuous feast our chef has prepared for us."

"May our journey be as fine and delightful as the food we are about to eat." The captain raised his glass, "To you, my honored guests, without you none of this would be possible."

For the appetizer, Henry and Bella placed on the golden charger before each guest, a delicate bone china plate with a small circle of baked mashed potatoes, topped with lobster, and crowned in caviar. Each dish presented was elegantly plated with food that melted in the mouth, dazzling the taste buds. Dessert was a flambé vanilla-poached pear drizzled with apricot sauce.

Throughout the meal, Charlie appreciated the subtle unfurling of clues. He observed Sophia's hand disappearing under the table; each time the first officer's eyes widened and Peter's narrowed. He empathized with Jack, who grew more uncomfortable with each double entendre his sister moaned. Bella's obvious fascination with Peter Ferguson, and Henry's apparent distaste for the man piqued Charlie's curiosity. Even more provoking was one of the female guests, sitting next to the captain, and her obvious preoccupation with the Sophia and Peter show at the opposite end of the table. Charlie remembered overhearing the captain introducing the woman and her husband to Marian as Kay and Ethan Tolbert.

Charlie was pleased with Marian's refined interrogation of Peter, each question leading to another, seamlessly gathering information, every soothing laugh easing any tensions. But Sophia, on the other hand, was focused on the first officer, only offering shallow answers to Marian's questions, if even answering at all, too absorbed in seducing the handsome, young officer.

Squeezing Marian's knee, Charlie winked at her and nodded toward Sophia, and then he moved to sit next to Sophia, rescuing the embarrassed first officer.

"Sophia, so tell me, are you and Peter going dancing after dinner?"

Her eyes shifted between Peter, the first officer, Marian, and then back to Charlie's green eyes. She leaned toward Charlie, her shoulder a hair's breadth between them, and then smiled hesitantly, her eyes shifted toward Marian, not knowing how far she could go without annoying Marian. Sophia distanced herself from Charlie, focusing her attention now on Peter.

"Peter, do you dance?" Sophia reached across the table for his hand.

So, she doesn't know him that well. Charlie cleared his throat, "Peter, you should join Marian and me on the dance floor." Charlie slapped Jack on the back. "You're coming, right?"

"The fifth wheel? No, thanks," Jack sat back, away from the table.

Marian clicked her tongue, "Jack, you don't have to dance; we enjoy your company. Besides you already promised, remember?"

"The boy dances better than me." Sophia declared. "Our mother made us go to the Arthur Murray Dance School with her and Dad. You should see his hips move."

Jack cringed. "What can I say? Our mother was very persuasive. You never said no to her or else—," Jack slapped the space in front of his face. "I figured if I had to be there; I might as well make the best of it."

Henry and Bella walked around the table, each had a tray of cordial glasses sweating with ice-cold Limoncello. Peter stood and removed one from the tray Bella was carrying, his gaze lingered on her full lips. Peter saluted the pretty maid and then sipped the sweet liqueur. "Just what I need." He turned his attention toward the table. "Let's hit the dance floor and show these newlyweds some moves."

Sophia giggled as she threaded her arm around Peter's. "Let me have one of these first." She leered at Henry as she knocked back the drink.

"Thank you for saving me," First Officer Cornelia whispered to Charlie.

With two fingers, Charlie saluted the relieved man. "Been there. No need to thank me."

The captain stood, and again, expressed his appreciation to the small group. Most of the guests remained with the captain and his officers, including the woman who had been fascinated with Peter and Sophia.

Marian pleaded with Jack, "You are coming with us?"

"Yeah, I need a relief man. This woman will dance me to death."
Charlie grinned, "What do you say, wiggle hips?"

Jack grinned at Marian and then sneered at Charlie, playfully
poking the detective's chest. "For you, no." He then helped Marian
from her chair. "But I will gladly go for you. Besides, I did promise
you earlier. Charlie can guard your clutch while we dance the night
away."

Charlie rolled his eyes. "Oh, brother."

♣

Charlie was happy to see the room filled with people. He enjoyed
dancing with Marian but felt more comfortable on a crowded dance
floor. There was a man and a woman on stage singing *Endless Love*.

Marian herded her small group to a vacant table next to the dance
floor, off to the side of the orchestra. Charlie's curiosity was aroused
as he watched her take a small slip of paper from her dainty black
clutch and pass it to the waiter taking their drink order.

The waiter casually handed the strip of paper to a band member.
When the band finished playing, the duet was given the paper. The
pair beamed. Looking around the crowd, they nodded at Marian who
was discreetly waving her hand.

"This song is dedicated to Charlie by Marian," announced the male
singer. The orchestra began to play as the duet waved Charlie and
Marian to the dance floor.

The duet began to sing, *At Last.* The crowd on the dance floor parted as Charlie and Marian made their way to the center of the dance floor.

"I love you, Charlie McClung," Marian whispered as she rested her head on his shoulder.

Charlie kissed the top of her ear. "I love you, too, sweetheart, more than I can put into words." Resting his face on the side of her head, he wanted to keep her safe, to make her feel secure in his love. The warmth of her breath on his neck felt like a sweet caress.

He searched the crowded room for any hints of danger, knowing there was a murderer on board made him feel uneasy, very uneasy for Marian now that she seemed to be a target for anyone he was searching for. Charlie's eyes glazed at the thought of almost losing her twice before and he held her tighter.

He saw a few familiar faces in the crowded room but the most curious one was that of the woman, Kaye, who had been sitting next to the captain. Her glare was fixed on Peter Ferguson. *What is her problem with Peter?* And then there was Henry lurking in shadows and Bella, who was now serving drinks to Sophia, Jack, and Peter. *What happened to our waiter?* Peter said something to Bella, making her giggle and Henry scowl. Charlie didn't want to be preoccupied with murder on his honeymoon, but then again, he had to keep Marian safe.

Charlie didn't need Jack to tell him that Tammy had been murdered. It was more than obvious, overkill to say the least. What worried him, was to what length the killer would go to keep from being caught. He pulled Marian in closer, kissed the top of her head, while the instinct to protect her burned in his gut. Closing his eyes, he said a prayer for the wisdom to catch the murderer quickly and to keep Marian from all harm, so they could enjoy their honeymoon free from any distractions.

For now, Charlie felt safe and he kept his eyes closed, enjoying the warmth of Marian's body and the feeling of her heartbeat on his chest. The music ended. Charlie looked around. The dance floor was empty and the crowd applauded them.

Marian stood on her toes. With both of her hands, she pulled Charlie's face toward hers and kissed him tenderly. "Thank you for loving me."

"Wait here." Charlie strode toward the duet and whispered into the man's ear.

He returned to his bride and placed his hands on the curve of her waist as the singer began to sing *My Girl*.

"Oh, Charlie, you're the best," Marian sighed.

Charlie looked surprised. "You're just figuring that out?"

Marian rolled her eyes and groaned as she wrapped her arms around him.

At the end of the song, the band announced a five-minute break. Making their way back to the table, Charlie noticed Jack sitting alone, his hand protecting two black clutches. He then noticed Sophia talking to a few of the band members. Scanning the packed room, he saw Peter standing in the double-wide doorway with Kaye Tolbert in a heated discussion, at least, she appeared to be angry. Peter had an "I couldn't care less" smug look on his face.

Charlie was itching to interrogate the mounting suspects but not tonight. Tonight belonged to Marian.

"Marian, would you like something to drink? Jack?" Charlie asked, noticing Jack's drained beer mug.

"Well, if you're buying, I'll have another beer."

"An ice-cold beer sounds good to me, too," Marian agreed with Jack as she fanned herself with her clutch.

Charlie headed to the bar, luckily it was very close to the doorway where Peter and Kaye were having their conversation. As he waited for the three beers he had ordered, Charlie took a few discreet steps in their direction. He could only hear a few words over the ambient noise, but the words he did hear, coupled with Kaye's tone, made it clear she was most displeased with Peter.

Kaye raised her hand as if she were going to slap the cocky grin off of Peter's face, instead, she stormed away, almost running into Charlie.

The bartender waved to Charlie. Peter sauntered next to Charlie as he was signing the check. "Hey, no! Bartender, throw this away." Peter snatched the paper from underneath the ink pen, wading it into a tiny ball. "Put his drinks on my tab and add a boilermaker and a Sex on the Beach to it."

"Thanks, Peter, but you don't have to do that." Charlie could smell the alcohol on his breath and was surprised at how well Peter was functioning.

"What's the point of having money if you can't spend it on the people you like? And I like you, McClung." Peter winked as he clicked his tongue and pointed his finger.

"Here ya go, sir, your boilermaker and cocktail."

A waiter set a tray of empty glasses on the bar next to Peter.

Peter grabbed the waiter's shoulder. "Be a sport and bring these drinks to that table." He pointed toward their table and then handed the young man a twenty. "Follow me, son."

Once at the table, Peter leered at Sophia, "Here's a drink for you."

Sophia accepted the cocktail from him. "Mmm, my favorite, Sex on the Beach."

Jack looked at the ceiling, and then with a groan, dropped his gaze to his lap.

The band started playing, *I'm a Believer*.

Sophia jumped up, pulling up Jack with her. "Come dance with me, like we used to," she pleaded.

"Wouldn't you rather have Peter?"

Sophia stomped her foot. "No! Don't you remember this song?"

"Fine!"

Jack followed his sister. The pair began to dance, their shakes and shimmies perfectly synchronized to the music.

"Come on, let's join them," Marian shouted as she hiked up her dress and danced her way toward Jack and Sophia.

Charlie looked at Peter and shrugged. "Why not?"

Determined not to be outshined, the two men joined the trio and began to gyrate, legs and arms flaying about like dying snakes, making a spectacle of themselves, and stealing the show.

Chapter 7

Charlie and Marian planned to explore the vast ship, looking for a nice hideaway to talk about the events of last night. The day was a bit overcast, not a good day to lounge by the pool. The suite was exquisite but they wanted to keep it for honeymoon talk, not murder and mayhem.

He watched Marian put the finishing touches to her wandering outfit, as she had called it. She slid onto her thin wrist, a wide, silver-filigree dragonfly cuff bracelet. The phone rang as she leaned toward the dresser mirror to apply plum-colored lip gloss.

Charlie saw Marian watching his reflection in the mirror and he watched her face as she tried to interpret his side of the conversation.

"What's the matter?" She asked as he hung up the phone.

Charlie rubbed his thumb gently across her furrowed brow. "Nothing's wrong. I promised I would always give you all the facts, right?"

"Yes."

He put his hands on the curve of her waist, one of his many favorite spots. "Well, you know there's going to be an investigation into Tammy Ferguson's death and I'm a part of it."

Marian shook her head, "We're a part of it, me and you. The both of us. I thought that's what we were going to do, find a place to discuss *our* findings in the investigation, right?"

Charlie hit his forehead with the heel of his hand. "I forgot."

"Ha, ha, you're so funny," Marian replied sarcastically. "So, what does that phone call have to do with it?"

"Well, my little Mata Hari, that was Officer Watson, he wants me," Charlie saw Marian's left eyebrow arch, "I mean, us, to attend a briefing about Tammy's death. Jack and Doctor Nelson will be at the meeting, too. They've finished the autopsy, well, the best they could with the limited resources onboard."

Marian smiled and kissed him. "When?"

"In an hour."

She grabbed Charlie's wrist and looked at his watch. "What will we do about lunch?"

"That … well … mmm, it's a working lunch and there'll be discussions about the autopsy, a lot of it. Do you think you can handle that?"

Her mouth twisted as she thought about it. "Well, I've been eating like a little piglet, so maybe a light lunch would do me good."

The doorbell rang, followed by a soft knock on the door.

"Henry, what can I do for you?"

"I am so sorry to disturb you and madam, but I have a delivery of flowers from Mr. Ferguson for madam."

Charlie took note of Henry's painful expression when he said, *Mr. Ferguson.*

"Thank you, Henry," Marian stepped beside Charlie. She reached for the bouquet of yellow and white daisies.

"If madam would like, I will place them on your dresser for you."

Charlie and Marian stepped aside for Henry, who was determined to do his job.

"Mr. McClung, sir, please do not take offense when I say that madam is worthy of roses." Seeing their confused expression, Henry added, "But I do believe any gesture of kindness is generous." He looked at the daisies, "No matter how small the token is."

Marian smiled. "Yes, Henry, you're right. Thank you."

Henry bowed slightly. "Is there anything at all that you require?"

She read the small card attached to the flowers, *Thank you for helping me forget my woes and for not judging me. Peter,* and then passed it to Charlie.

He grunted when he read the note, tossed it into the trash, and then asked Henry, "Why, yes, there is. Surely, you know every inch of this ship."

"Yes, sir, intimately."

Charlie cleared his throat and gestured between himself and Marian, "We are looking for a secluded area where we can talk. You know what I mean?"

Henry nodded. "I know the perfect place. At this time of day, in the library, there is a nook that is scarcely used. Shall I show you, while Bella cleans your room?"

Charlie heard Bella's cleaning cart bang against an outside wall.

"Sure! Marian are you ready?"

Marian snatched a grass-woven beach tote, the one Charlie called her basket purse, from the coffee table. "I'm ready."

They followed Henry down the corridor, into an elevator, down a few decks, then down another corridor, and into the library. A tall, silver-haired woman stood perusing the bookshelves with one hand resting on her ample hip, while the other hand skimmed the spines of the books, and was completely unaware of their presence.

Henry led them to the private sitting area. "May I bring you anything to drink or eat? Perhaps coffee and a basket of Tuscan lemon muffins?"

"Oh, yum! Please, if it's no trouble."

Henry flashed a smile, "Not at all, madam. Not at all."

Charlie patted Henry's shoulder, a very muscular shoulder. "You're too good to her, Henry. I may have to bring you home with us." He felt Henry tense up.

"Not at all, sir, I am here to serve and respect your every wish." With a tight smile, Henry nodded, "Shall I bring you anything else?"

"No, Henry, the coffee and muffins will be splendid," Marian replied. "Thank you for showing us this little nook."

"No problem, madam. I will return shortly."

Charlie watched Henry leave, then followed him to make sure Henry was on his way down the corridor and to verify the book perusing lady was gone, too.

"He's one odd duck."

Marian smirked, "Yeah, rather peculiar but I can't quite put my finger on exactly why." She shrugged her shoulders, "Oh, well, let's compare our notes on last night."

"You first." Charlie slid his arm around Marian's shoulders.

"Well, Sophia and Peter work for the same company, for about three years now. And he said that it was a surprise that she was onboard."

Charlie kissed her on the cheek. "Sorry, going to need both hands," he said as he removed a notepad and pen from his shirt pocket. "Need to ask Jack when he made reservations and when he asked his sister to come with him. And check with Watson to see if he can find out when Peter Ferguson made his reservation."

Marian snickered. "Sounds good, Sherlock."

Smiling Charlie replied, "He's Watson and I'm Sherlock. I bet he's heard that a million times."

"Sorry, I couldn't resist."

"Shall we continue? Did you notice the lady at the end of the dining table last night, the one giving Peter and Sophia the evil eye?

Marian was startled by Henry's silent entrance.

He deftly set down a silver tray with the promised muffins and coffee. "Shall I pour?"

"Thank you but Marian and I can handle it. I'm sure you have more pressing things to do than to wait on us."

"Very well, I hope you and madam have a nice afternoon." Henry seemed to float out of the room.

Charlie asked again as he poured a cup of coffee for Marian, "Did you notice the woman?"

Marian held up a finger as she swallowed a chunk of muffin. "Yes, weird wasn't it? I wanted to speak with her but I got so caught up with all the talk about dancing; I completely forgot about her."

"There's something going on between the two of them. When I went to the bar to get our drinks, I saw them arguing. She was doing most of the talking. Peter had a "yeah, whatever" look."

Marian added a generous amount of creamer to her coffee and then snagged another muffin, carefully peeling away its lace-like paper liner. "You know Bella has a crush on Peter, and Henry doesn't like it."

"Oh, yeah, how do you know?"

"Yesterday, when I went to our cabin to get ready for dinner, Bella was tidying up. She was going to leave because I was there but I told her to finish because I would be in the bathroom showering. While I was in there, before getting into the shower, Henry came in and began to chastise her for not having our cabin cleaned. Then they argued about Peter. Evidently, Bella and Henry had a relationship at one point.

And …" Marian paused.

Charlie yawned.

"Yeah, yeah, yeah, I see the "look". Long story short, Henry knows Bella is after Peter and doesn't approve of her behavior. He even pushed her onto the bed."

"Has a temper, does he?" Charlie made a note of it.

Marian puffed her cheeks and exhaled loudly. "Do you really know that Tammy was murdered?"

"My detective sense says yes, but Jack will tell us for sure." Charlie stood, "Enough cop talk. I need some us time. Let's stroll around the shops before we head to the meeting to find that out for sure." He extended his hand toward Marian, who gladly accepted. Pulling her to his chest, Charlie wrapped his arms around her and inhaled the scent of her neck. "Mmm, I sure do love you. I won't let anything happen to you, ever."

Painful memories stumbled suddenly around in her mind. Marian held him tighter, with each beat of his heart, the memories faded away. "I know, Charlie. I can feel it. My love for you is unfathomable." She looked up at him, afraid she might cry. "Kiss me, and then buy me something pretty."

Charlie stared into her glassy eyes, knowing she was on the verge of tears, kissed her, then replied, "As you wish."

Chapter 8

Charlie and Marian were the last to arrive at the meeting to discuss Tammy Ferguson's death. Doctor Nelson and Officer Watson were mildly surprised to see Marian.

"See, I told you guys she'd be here." Jack was studying the buffet loaded with too much food for just five people before he made his final selections.

"No way to hold her back when there's a good mystery at hand," Charlie shrugged and made his way to the buffet.

Marian frowned, "I hope it's not a problem. I do have information that I think is meaningful to the investigation. And don't worry, Charlie already warned me the autopsy report would be read and discussed."

Officer Watson smiled, "No problem at all. The more facts we have the better." He lightly touched her elbow, leading her to the buffet. "Please, help yourself, the chef has outdone himself again."

"Can we go ahead and get this meeting started? The more time we have the better, who knows when I'll be called out for a medical emergency." Doctor Nelson sat down and began to eat. "I have copies of my report for everyone," he nodded toward a stack of papers in the center of the conference table.

Charlie read the report as he ate a grilled ham and cheese sandwich. "Marian, one more warning, this is graphic."

"That's why I'm drinking ginger ale and only eating crackers, for now." She sat next to her husband, retrieved a copy of the autopsy report and thought, *it couldn't be any worse than Dianne Pannell's, at least there's no bullet holes or blood involved.*

Jack scratched his narrow chin, "Let's see, after conferring with Doctor Nelson, who has asked me to take lead on this, it is our conclusion that Tammy Ferguson was murdered and we put the time of death around eleven o'clock last night."

"Why?" Marian asked as she drummed her fingertips on the unread autopsy report.

Charlie held her hand, stopping her nervous tapping.

Jack was amused by her question. "We're going to go over our findings, although we couldn't do a complete autopsy, the ship is not equipped for that, all of the external evidence supports our decision."

"Let's all look at page two," Doctor Nelson instructed.

Kissing Marian's hand, Charlie released it so she could follow along.

"I'll get straight to the pertinent facts. There is a significant rash around the mouth, chin, neck, and hands. The rash is obvious inside her mouth, including the gums and tongue. Her face, eyes, lips, fingers on the right hand, and tongue are swollen as well as the throat, enough to close off her airway and cause asphyxiation."

From underneath his copy of the autopsy report, Jack retrieved a large brown envelope and took out eleven 8 x 11 color pictures. He handed one of the pictures to Officer Watson. "As you can see from the first photo, a close-up of the victim's face, the reaction was severe."

Watson's eyes widened, not expecting the freakishly bizarre image of Tammy's grotesquely swollen lips and eyelids. Next, he was handed a photo of the inside of her mouth; teeth marks were visible on her thick, rash-covered tongue that had been pressed firmly against her teeth. He was then given three close-ups of her neck and both hands. Her neck had faint bruising, slight scratch marks, and a smattering of rash. The rash on her hands was more apparent, running down her fingers and knuckles like a lava flow. The left index finger was twice its normal size. Officer Watson passed the photos to Charlie.

"Marian, these pictures are quite graphic. Have you ever seen someone who's had a severe allergic reaction before?" Charlie laid the photos face down and placed his hands on top of them to prevent Marian from taking them.

She sighed, "I'm not a delicate little, hot-house flower. And yes, my father was allergic to bees. Once a bee stung him on the lip and it was so swollen it looked like it was turned inside out." Marian held out her hand for the photos.

"All right then, be my guest but there's a bit more involved than a swollen lip."

Marian was determined not to flinch at whatever she saw. The first two were of Tammy's hands, easy to handle; the one of her mouth was a bit more severe. Seeing the progression of the photos, she knew the last one would be the worst. Her gasp was immediate at the sight of Tammy's unrecognizable face. "What caused this?"

Charlie removed the photo from Marian's trembling hand, passing it back to Jack.

"Suffocation caused by anaphylactic shock, the swelling of her tongue and throat cut off her air supply. Now, as far as what she came into contact with to cause the severe anaphylactic reaction, well, I'm still working on that but we do have a theory which I'll get to later. Hopefully, Charlie will discover who administered it and why."

"Hopefully?" Charlie laughed, "Come on, Jack, you know I can."

Jack shifted his gaze toward Marian then back to Charlie. "I have no doubt that you're capable of solving the murder, but Charlie, you're on your honeymoon. How can you … you know … do both?"

"My husband is quite talented," Marian said bluntly.

The men stared at her, not sure how to respond to her comment. Charlie grinned, slid his arm around her shoulders, and said, "Thank you, my dear, with you by my side, we can do anything." He kissed her temple. "My darling bride has talents, too. She can get people to open up to her without realizing they're being interrogated."

Officer Watson coughed. "All right then, Charlie will conduct the investigation however he sees fit. Is there any more evidence that you would like to present?"

"Yes, these last pictures of the victim's legs." Jack passed them to Watson. "There is a bruise on her left thigh. It appears to have been made within seconds of her death as if someone kicked her. The right upper area of the thigh has a rectangular bruise that was probably caused when she banged against the door frame."

Marian looked perplexed. "How do you know she was dead when she received the bruise on her left thigh?"

"Good question and easy to answer, the coloring of the bruises are markedly different." Jack then passed around two more photos, full body shots, front and back. "As you can see, there are no distinguishing marks except for a few moles and an oval-shaped birthmark on her right buttock and there are no other injuries."

Marian was happy to see that Jack had respect for the dead; her intimate parts were covered. She studied the bruises on Tammy's thighs, noticing the distinctively different shades and shapes of the two bruises.

Leaning forward, Jack slid two pictures toward the middle of the small table and then tapped a spot on each one. "Here is an unusual mark found on her upper gum and again here on her finger."

They all strained to see the spots. Doctor Nelson produced a magnifying glass. "This will help."

Charlie took the magnifier and the pictures. "Hmm, a puncture wound, a needle? Was she diabetic; I don't remember seeing any needles lying around the cabin?" He looked at Officer Watson, "I've got to get back into that cabin, now before anything more is disturbed."

"No need to worry about that. Doctor Nelson was quick-thinking and had the suite locked down. No one has entered the cabin since last night."

On his way to the buffet for seconds, Jack answered, "No, she was not diabetic."

Charlie nodded, "That's good. So, we know Tammy died from anaphylactic shock. She has two puncture wounds, one to her gum and one to her left index finger, but we don't know what caused the puncture wounds. And I would venture to guess that whatever made the wounds is what was used to administer the unknown toxin."

Everyone agreed.

"Jack, Doctor Nelson, what kind of poison would cause that kind of damage?" Charlie retrieved his notepad and pen, prepared to make notes.

The two doctors looked at one another. Doctor Nelson nodded quickly toward Jack to answer.

"Almost anything can be an allergen: nuts, seafood, dust mites, pollen, certain drugs, the lists goes on and on and remember, reactions to any allergen differs from person to person. It's really hard to say what it was for Tammy Ferguson." Jack sat down. "If we had the right equipment, we could run tests and find out." He held up a green olive. "Even this could be deadly."

Charlie scratched the back of his neck. "The husband said she was mildly allergic to peanuts and shellfish but avoided them like the plague. Can someone's tolerance change over the years?"

"Oh, absolutely!" Both doctors answered.

Tugging his earlobe, Charlie said, "I've got a lot to do in just a little time. First thing to do is search the cabin. Second, begin interviews."

"I think we also need to interview that woman at the captain's dinner. You know the one staring down Peter; I think her name was Kaye Tolbert." Marian looked at Jack. "Do you know her?"

Jack smirked, "No, I thought she was annoyed with my sister's rude behavior. You think it was Peter she was irritated with?"

"I saw Peter and her having what appeared to be a heated discussion near the bar last night." Charlie made a few more notes. "These are the people I want to interview, Peter Ferguson, Henry, Bella, Sophia, and Kaye Tolbert.

"Watson, will you contact everyone and arrange interview times? And speaking of interviews, can I use this room to conduct them and of course, I want you present for all of them."

Officer Watson grinned, "Bob's your uncle! Shall we begin …" He studied his watch, "at three o'clock? That'll give us close to three hours to search the room and prepare our strategy for the interviews. Who would you like first?"

"Peter Ferguson, then Bella, Sophia, Henry, and that woman, Kaye Tolbert. Depending on what we find out, there could be more to interview." Charlie slapped his thighs. "Well, let's get started. Doctor Nelson, can you supply us a few pairs of latex gloves for the search?"

Marian clicked her tongue, "Well, what about me? Am I invited to help search the cabin?"

"But of course, I want you to go through Tammy's things, see if there's anything unusual."

"I'll get gloves for everyone here. Oh, and don't forget to include Antonio Caruso on your list of people to interview."

"Who is that?" Charlie scribbled down the name.

Doctor Nelson's forehead wrinkled, "You should've been introduced upon your arrival. He's the concierge for the suites. Caruso is the one who alerted me about Tammy Ferguson."

Charlie and Officer Watson stared at one another, blinked, and then Charlie asked, "Why are you just telling us now that Antonio Caruso was the first to find the body, not her husband?"

Doctor Nelson shrugged. "I didn't think about it until now. Her condition and Peter's reaction overwhelmed me. I mean, at the time I had no idea she was dead, much less murdered." He took a sip of coffee. "Caruso informed me that she had passed out and was unresponsive, that's all."

"Is it normal for a concierge to be in someone's cabin at that time of night?" Charlie looked to Officer Watson for the answer.

"Guests call on the butlers, concierges, and guest services at all times of the day and night, so no, it's not out of the norm."

Marian interrupted. "So you're telling us that Peter was not in the cabin when she died." She blotted the corners of her eyes with a linen napkin. "How horrible."

Doctor Nelson shook his head. "He arrived shortly after I did."

"Where was he?" Charlie asked as he rubbed Marian's back.

"You'll have to ask him. My concern at the time was Tammy, and then Peter's well-being after I pronounced her dead."

Charlie closed the notepad and stood. "The sooner we start, the sooner we get to the answer." He held out his hand. "My dear, ready to snoop?"

"Yep, let's go."

Chapter 9

Officer Phillip Watson slid in the card key and opened the door, leading the way into the Ferguson's suite. It was dark and silent, an air of sickness seemed to float from the bathroom. The cabin had not been cleaned since that night. Everything remained the same. The beautiful floral arrangements, drooped, petals scattered about the table and floor, curled like dead spiders, the once green stems were tinged with brown, and the water in the vases was murky with decay.

"Let me go first, so I can get pictures of everything before we begin the search." The flash of the camera illuminated the short entryway before Officer Watson stepped inside. He took several shots of the bathroom, then motioned for them to enter, taking pictures as he ventured further into the suite.

"Jack, you and I will search the bathroom, since we suspect that's where she came into contact with the allergen. Doctor Nelson, you and Marian search the suite. If you find anything, and I mean anything that's strange, out of place, or of interest, have Watson get pictures before you move it. Okay?"

Everyone nodded.

"We'll join you once we've cleared the bathroom."

Charlie studied the chaos on the small vanity: jars of makeup, perfume, and creams had been pushed to one side. Everything seemed to be the same as it was when he first saw it on the night Tammy was killed, except the water had been turned off. The mirror looked like a piece of abstract art in dried toothpaste spatters.

"It had to be the toothpaste or something in the toothpaste. What do you think, Jack?" Charlie leaned over to get a closer view of the toothbrush lying next to the sink. He touched it with his index finger, rolled it over on its side, making the bristles point upward. There were dark specs embedded in the brush head.

Jack was examining the tube of toothpaste, the bottom half neatly pressed flat. "I would agree."

"What do you make of this?" Charlie pointed to the speckled toothbrush head.

"Trail mix from the coffee table, maybe? I'll bag it. There's a pretty powerful microscope in the clinic."

Charlie made a note to ask Peter about the trail mix. "From the looks of things in here, I'd say this is where she went into shock." Leaning his head outside the bathroom, he called out, "Watson, will you come get a few pictures of some items before we bag them?" He pointed to the toothbrush and the toothpaste.

Officer Watson took pictures from various angles before the items were bagged. "Anything else?"

"The mirror and the sink as well." Charlie stood in the bathroom doorway. There was a bluish smudge shoulder-high on the doorframe. "And this, too."

Stepping out of Watson's way, Charlie examined the walls just outside of the bathroom. One of them had an odd shading waist-high.

"Get a picture of this. I think this is where Tammy fell to her knees and pressed against this wall to get up."

Charlie followed the path that Tammy seemed to have taken. The mattress was crooked. *She must have hit the corner before she collapsed to the floor.* The telephone sat on the nightstand on the other side of the bed. "She never made it." He pointed at the phone.

"What did you say?" Marian looked over her shoulder, her husband was deep in thought. She abandoned the dresser drawer she had been searching, and lightly touched Charlie's forearm.

"I'm sorry dear, did you say something?" Charlie stood with his hands on his hips as he scanned the room.

Marian took the same stance and followed his gaze. "Yes, I did. I asked you what you said or rather mumbled."

Charlie saw the trail mix, a bottle of merlot, and two wine glasses on the coffee table. "Watson, please get a picture of all of this and bag some of the trail mix. And to answer your question, my love, I think Tammy ran into the corner of bed on her way to the telephone but collapsed and died before she could reach it. See here." He pointed to the misaligned mattress. "And the duvet is bunched up on the floor."

Doctor Nelson stood by Charlie. "Yep, that's where she was when I entered the room. Peter was kneeling next to her, patting her face, and begging her to wake up."

"So, if Peter was here, why did this Caruso guy get you? Why didn't Peter call for help?" Charlie motioned for Jack to follow him to the coffee table.

"I'm not sure why. Caruso banged on my cabin door, told me about Mrs. Ferguson, led me to their suite, and then disappeared."

Charlie bagged a handful of the trail mix. "Jack, you think this might be the cause?" He turned and looked at Doctor Nelson. "Don't you think that's rather odd, for him to get you and not Peter?"

Doctor Nelson rubbed the back of his head. "Now that I think about it, yeah, it's odd, very odd. So, now I'm wondering who found Mrs. Ferguson first?"

"And why was Caruso here at all?" Charlie made a few more notes. "We've got to get a timeline on how all of this went down." He looked at his watch. "It's one-thirty. I think we're about finished here. Did anyone find anything of interest?"

"Yeah, she had a drawer with some interesting undergarments." Marian crossed her arms and looked around the suite. "Doctor Nelson, what was she wearing when you found her? Did she still have on her makeup, was her hair still fixed, was she wearing perfume?"

"Yes to all of your questions and she was wearing one of our robes and ..." Doctor Nelson searched for the correct word. "I guess, it's called a G-string or thong? Not something I would've thought she'd be wearing. Now, that's just my opinion, of course."

"That's all she was wearing? What color was it, the thong, I mean?" Marian stared at the pale blue nightgown crumpled on the bed.

"Pale blue."

"Well, I don't know about all women, but I'd never go to sleep wearing a thong. Those are for ..." Marian blushed. She had forgotten that she was standing in a room with men other than her husband. She coughed. "Anyway, she must have been expecting someone, that's all I'm saying."

"I'll bag the nightgown." Charlie neatly folded the sheer negligée. "Nothing like a woman's point of view, invaluable, and I honestly mean that, Marian."

She kissed his cheek. "Thank you."

Officer Watson chuckled, "Maybe I should hire a female deputy? I wouldn't mind a peck or two, every now and then."

Charlie slid his arm around Marian's waist and in an Irish accent he replied, "Aye, but ya not be havin' as fine a lass as this one!"

"Oh, please, I know you're on your honeymoon, but this is getting sickeningly sappy." Jack rubbed his naked ring finger.

Charlie removed his arm from Marian's waist, assuming a no-nonsense persona. "If she was waiting for someone, who was it, Peter or Antonio Caruso?" He tugged on his earlobe, deep in thought, then rubbed his hands together. "Watson, did you get pictures of everything?"

"All areas photographed, even took pictures inside the waste bins and under the furniture."

"Excellent! I think we've got it covered but I would still like this cabin off limits to everyone except us of course."

Officer Watson held up a card key. "No one can enter this suite unless they have this; the only one that works."

"Anyone have any questions or thoughts before we leave?" Charlie saw everyone shake their heads.

"Brilliant! I say let's get cracking on the plans for the interviews."

Chapter 10

The conference room was bright and cheery, set for afternoon tea even though it was only three o'clock. The buffet was complete with multiple three-tiered cake stands, each one layered with different savories and sweets. Pots of tea and coffee, bowls of clotted cream, lemon curd, jams, and marmalades, rounded out the epicurean display.

All the guests knew they were to be questioned about Tammy Ferguson's death, but Charlie was hoping it was enough of a disguise to lull the suspects into a sense of relaxation or feel this was an innocuous threat. The room was definitely a far cry from any interrogation room he'd ever seen.

Charlie was pouring a cup of coffee when Peter walked in, three o'clock on the dot. He held up the French press pot covered in a Harris Tweed cozy. "Cuppa?"

"Is it coffee or tea?"

"Coffee."

"Please." Peter perused the buffet. "Is this a party or an interrogation?" He tossed onto a china plate a few crustless sandwiches, a smoked salmon on pumpernickel and a caviar egg salad on white bread, and then shoved a cucumber sandwich into his mouth.

Charlie held up the creamer.

"I take my coffee in its natural state, black." Peter took the cup, sipping from it as he circled the small conference table. He pulled out a chair and sat facing Charlie who was standing next to the buffet.

Charlie smiled and walked over to the table, "Good coffee, huh?" He sat across from Peter, studying his body language.

"The best, but then again, I've always thought cruise ships have the best coffee."

"Is that right? This is my first cruise, Marian's too. How many have you taken?"

Peter screwed his mouth, drumming his fingers against the china cup as he thought about the question and then shook his head. "I've lost count. We've been cruising since we married, at least once a year sometimes two or three times. They begin to run together."

"Married thirty-five years, that's a lot of cruises. Always book on the same cruise line?

Returning to the buffet, Peter tossed onto his plate, a mini custard tart and a couple of ginger fairings, topped off his coffee, and then sat down. "We tried all of them, well that is, the upper-class ones. That's how Tammy refers …referred to them." He dunked a ginger fairing into his coffee. "Then Tammy decided this one suited her best, so we've cruised on this one for the past thirty years or so."

Charlie made a note.

"Where did that come from?"

"This notepad?"

Peter nodded.

"I always have one with me. I'm a copper."

Peter chuckled. "Well, that's a term from the past, copper. McClung. That's Irish, right?"

"Yes. I come from a long line of coppers." Charlie was pleased that Peter was feeling at ease with him.

Officer Phillip Watson entered the room. "So sorry. I was a tad bit delayed, work you know." He poured a cup of tea and splashed in some cream. Sitting next to Charlie, he slid the chair away from the table and casually crossed his legs. "Shall we begin?"

Charlie cringed inside as he witnessed Peter stiffen when Watson said, *Shall we begin*, and he protectively held his cup with both hands, appearing to be ready to bolt at any given moment. *I guess it has been a while since Watson interviewed anyone. Just when I had Peter feeling like just one of the guys.*

Leaning back into his chair, Charlie relaxed with a sigh and took a drink of coffee. "You're right about this coffee, Peter. I don't believe I've ever had a better cup. But don't tell my Ma." He saw Peter's body release a little bit of tension as he snorted at Charlie's remark.

"Yeah, I know what you mean. My Tammy doesn't … didn't even cook but she got mad whenever I complimented another woman's cooking." Peter's frown was sad as he thought about his dead wife.

Charlie leaned in a little. "You must've loved her a lot to be married for thirty-five years."

"Yeah." Peter shrugged. "Our marriage was…" he bobbed his head side to side, "it was different but solid."

"What do you mean by different?" Charlie drained his cup.

Peter reached for the empty cup. "Would you like another one?"

Charlie shook his head. "Thanks, not right now. Different, how?"

"Well, at first it was a typical marriage but after a few years and no kids, mmm, we kinda became best friends." Peter scratched behind his ear. "I mean we loved each other, I mean truly loved each other, supported each other, but we developed different interests."

Officer Watson stood up silently, went to the buffet and returned with the coffee pot, refilled everyone's cup, including his own, without asking.

Peter scowled at Watson. "Thank you. Does this mean I'll be here for a while?" He held up the cup of steaming coffee.

"No, not at all. I only have a few more questions." Charlie made note of Peter's annoyance with Officer Watson and decided to cut to the chase. "When you say developed different interests, do you mean other people? An open marriage?"

His face reddened but Peter nodded.

"But you say Tammy was aware of your dalliances and you of hers. She had her own, too, I suppose."

Peter seemed shocked. "Well, I … uh … really don't know."

"Don't know if she knew of yours or if she had her own sex life without you?"

Peter opened his mouth and then clamped shut, sitting in silence.

After a few seconds, Charlie continued. "I see. You have no idea if she did but she was aware of yours. Is that right?"

"I'm not comfortable talking about this." Peter stood.

"Please, Peter, just a couple more questions and I promise you can go and enjoy the rest of your cruise."

Peter looked at Charlie's innocent smile and sat down. "Look, let me explain. Tammy was my world. Everyone else was just a passing fancy. And she knew that."

"Okay, so why, if she meant that much to you, did you stray?" Charlie shifted a little more forward.

Peter wiped sweat from his forehead. "I don't know. Why are you asking these questions? What does this have to do with her death?"

"Because Tammy was murdered."

Peter's face contorted. "No! What?" His head swung toward Officer Watson then back to Charlie. "And you think I did it?" Air puffed from his lips as he tried to form a sentence. "I wasn't even there when it happened. Ask Bell …" Peter's mouth froze as a confused look transformed his angry face.

"Bella, the maid? Were you with her?" Charlie scribbled on the pad. "What time were you with her and where?"

Peter nodded. "Yeah, but it wasn't planned. I mean, I just happened to be in the Stargazer lounge and Bella shows up."

"How did she know you were there?" Charlie poked Watson's shoulder. "Is it normal for employees to fraternize with the guests?"

"They are not supposed to but I can't say it never happens. I'll check her schedule." Officer Watson wrote notes of his own on a legal pad.

Charlie asked Peter again. "How did she know you were there at that specific time? Did Tammy know?"

Peter shrugged. "I left the suite around nine-thirty but I have no idea how Bella knew where to find me. Tammy knew I'd be at a bar but not anyone in particular. I don't think she would've said anything to Bella. She didn't seem to care too much for the maid."

Charlie glanced at Peter. "Did she tell you that she didn't like Bella?"

"No, I say that because I ate one of the chocolates, the ones they put on your pillow at night. Anyway, I tossed the wrapper toward the trash can and missed. Tammy told me not to worry about it. She said, *that maid* can pick it up. Tammy didn't use Bella's name, just referred to her as *that maid*. And she said it like she had a bad taste in her mouth."

"Huh, so you left the wrapper on the floor?"

"Yep."

Charlie jotted down Peter's remarks. "So, let me get this right, night service had already turned down your bed, tidied up, and left chocolates on the pillows when you left the cabin to go to a bar?"

"Yes, we got back to our suite after dinner and a stroll around the promenade at around … I don't know … maybe around nine-fifteen."

"Why didn't Tammy go to the bar with you?"

"Tammy doesn't like noisy, crowded spaces like bars or concerts, the theater is okay for her but not places that can get rowdy." Peter grinned at the memory. "She said she was tired and wanted to read in bed."

Charlie nodded. "Was she still dressed when you left?"

"She had kicked off her shoes but other than that, yes."

"And she wasn't expecting anyone, room service maybe?

Peter frowned, "No. What are you getting at?"

"Nothing, just forming a timeline for housekeeping. You know, who may have entered the cabin after you left, that's all."

"May I go now?"

"One more question, Peter. Do you know of anyone who would want to harm Tammy?" Charlie studied Peter's face for the truth.

Peter shook his head as he stared past Charlie. "No. Tammy wasn't exactly the friendliest person but she was never intentionally mean to anyone, maybe a little rude every now and then if she felt she was being disrespected."

Charlie believed him. "I think that's all I need for now."

Peter stood and turned to leave.

"Oh, one other thing. How long have you known Sophia?"

He sat down. "This is going to be more than one question, isn't?"

"I'll do my best to make it quick." Charlie leaned forward. "So, how long have you known her?"

Peter tapped his long index finger on the table. "Around three years, maybe."

"How did you meet?"

"Work. We met at work. She's one of my best sales reps."

"I can see that," Office Watson replied sarcastically.

Peter glared at him. "You do what you have to do to make a sale." He paused. "Within reason, that is."

Charlie looked up from his notes. "You said, "one of my best sales reps," do you own the company?"

"I wish! We work for an international medical device company. I'm a regional manager."

"Did you know she was going to be on this cruise? I don't recall seeing her at your renewal ceremony." Charlie stared at Peter.

"She wasn't at the renewal ceremony because she wasn't invited and I didn't know she was on the ship until I bumped into her at the poolside bar." Peter placed his hands, fingers splayed, on the table. "Look, I know what you're hinting at. I'm not having an affair with Sophia. She's just divorced and wants to have some fun, that's all."

Charlie scratched his forehead. "I see. You're both sowing wild oats now that you're both single. I noticed you said that you weren't *having* an affair with her, but have you ever had an affair with Sophia?"

Peter grinned. "You like playing around with words don't you?"

Officer Watson interrupted, "Just answer the question."

"No. I don't sleep around with company employees." Peter rubbed his face with both hands. "Can I go now?"

Charlie held up one finger. "Just one more question. If she wasn't an employee, would you?"

"What?" Peter was flushed. "No, I'm too old for her."

"Is that what she said?"

Peter stood suddenly, pushing back his chair. "Why don't you ask her? Can I go now?"

"What did Tammy have for dinner?"

"Steak."

"Anything with garlic?"

"No, she wasn't a big fan of it. Can I go now?"

Charlie nodded and motioned him toward the door.

Chapter 11

Officer Watson waited for Peter's footfalls to disappear before he shut the conference door. So we know someone was in that room when Tammy died.

"Yes, and we know she was, more than likely, waiting for someone for something more than a chat, according to Marian."

Watson rubbed his chin. "Because of the underwear thing?"

"Mhm." Charlie tapped the notepad with his pen. "We know someone picked up the wrapper and tossed it into the trashcan. And we know someone kicked her just as she died."

Charlie dropped the pen as he stood and stretched. "So, Tammy was getting ready for someone. She took off her clothes and …" Charlie slapped his forehead. "I should have asked Peter about her underwear."

Watson choked a little on the finger sandwich he was eating. "How would you ask that? Peter, does your wife wear thong knickers all the time or just when she's going to shag you?" He shook his head. "Honestly? How are you going to ask him that?"

Charlie laughed. "I'll find a way, don't worry about that." He searched the buffet for clotted cream and strawberry jam to put on the scone on his plate. Once he found it, Charlie put a thick layer of each on the plain scone.

"Watson, did you think Peter seem disturbed by the thought that Tammy may have had lovers of her own?" Charlie licked jam from his fingers.

"I do believe you hit a nerve when you made that suggestion."

Charlie tugged his ear. "Maybe she was on a different team if you know what I mean?"

"What!" Officer Watson thought about it. "I wouldn't admit it if my wife changed teams, would you? I mean, it would be a bit of an ego buster to my manhood."

He couldn't imagine Marian ever changing teams. She was too … he couldn't go there or he'd have to quickly leave the room. Charlie tossed his hands into the air. "It's just a theory."

Officer Watson looked at his watch. "Bella should be here soon. I'm interested in learning why she fancies Peter. He's not what I would consider a handsome bloke, maybe it's his money?"

There was a solid rap on the door.

Marian popped her head into the room. "May I come in?" She stepped into the room, firmly closing the door.

Charlie crossed the room, planting a kiss on her cheek, and then walked her to the conference table. "Have some tea. We have a few minutes before Bella arrives." He set a cup of Earl Grey in front of his wife.

Marian innocently looked over the rim of the cup as she blew on the steaming tea. "So, what were you talking about?" She sat down the cup. "I mean, I know you interviewed Peter. Any surprises?" Her gaze settled on Charlie's beautiful green eyes. "Any theories, yet?"

"It's not nice to eavesdrop," Charlie teased.

"Ah, but you know as well as I do, that's the best way to develop theories. You'll thank me one day for my bat-like ears. I can't help it if I *overhear* things when a door is cracked open a wee bit."

"Well, Mrs. McClung …

Marian smirked. "Although I love being Mrs. McClung, please call me Marian, Officer Watson."

"As you wish, Marian. Why do you think Bella is interested in Peter Ferguson besides his money?"

"Maybe, she likes a father figure. When you question Bella, ask her about her father." Marian sipped the tea. "Or, she just likes to conquer any man who is a challenge to her. I've seen her flirting with Peter but he doesn't seem as enthused."

Charlie and Officer Watson looked at each other, shook their heads, and then said, "Women."

"Well, the same can be said for men. I mean, look at Peter, although he said he doesn't date employees, he sure is sniffing awfully hard around Sophia."

Charlie's eyebrows pulled together. "How long were you out there listening?"

"Mmm," she tapped her finger on her chin and stared at the ceiling as she thought, "the whole time." Marian stood, wandered to the buffet, chose a few finger sandwiches, and then turned to look at the two perplexed men. "Was that wrong?" She nibbled on a cucumber sandwich.

Charlie's tongue ran over his full lips as he thought about how to address her question. "Well, sweetie …"

Marian held up one finger. "Before you say anything, let me tell you how I see it."

"All right, go ahead."

"If this were a proper interview room, it would have a two-way mirror, right?"

"Yes." Charlie knew where Marian was going but let her finish her reasoning.

Marian offered to refill the two men's cups, both accepting. She continued as she poured out the coffee. "And you said, both of you agreed that I was part of this investigation. So the way I see it, I would have been on the other side of that two-way mirror not only watching but …" She tapped her petite right ear, "also listening, right?"

Charlie hung his head and sighed. "Man, am I glad you're on the right side of the law. Heaven help us all if you weren't."

"Aye, you have that right, McClung, but she'd make for a fine detective inspector."

There was a soft knock on the door.

"Shall I answer?" Marian looked at Charlie for permission.

"Yeah, it's more than likely Bella." He noticed his wife was about to speak but Charlie continued, "And if you don't mind, wait on the other side of the two-way mirror. I think Bella will be more at ease with just the two of us." He motioned between himself and Officer Watson.

She grinned, "You read my mind. Spooky. We're already acting like an old married couple."

Marian opened the door with Bella waiting on the other side. "Hello, Bella, I'm just leaving. Please come in."

The young girl smiled and swept by Marian as if she was eager to be alone with the two handsome, older men, and not at all worried they were two officers of the law about to question her concerning her possible involvement with the death of one of the guests. This was a game to her, a game of conquest, a game of cat and mouse.

Chapter 12

Charlie and Officer Watson stood to greet Bella, offering her tea and scones before they began the interview.

Puzzled by her carefree attitude, Charlie wanted to understand if she understood the seriousness of the situation. "Bella, you do know why we asked you to come speak with us today?"

"Yes," she smiled sweetly.

Charlie pursed his lips and thought *All right then, let's just jump straight into it without worrying about unsettling her.* "When was the last time you saw Tammy Ferguson alive?"

Bella picked at a blueberry scone, pushing bits of it into her mouth as she thought about the question. "Mmm, I don't know. Maybe as she and Peter, I mean, Mr. Ferguson left for dinner, maybe?"

"And about what time was that, five o'clock, seven o'clock?" Charlie stared unfeelingly at her.

Bella's smile faltered, unsure where she stood, her charm seemed to be ineffective on the two men. "Well, they went to an early dinner, older people tend to do that you know. So, I guess it was around five thirty."

Officer Watson shifted in his chair. "Was their cabin the first one you cleaned for the night?"

"I'm pretty sure the Ferguson's cabin was the third one I cleaned." Her hands smoothed the loose French braid wound around her head.

The auburn braid was lopsided, hanging down, covering her right ear. Bella's pensive green eyes seemed to sparkle as she stared at Officer Watson. Her smile strengthened, exposing her perfectly straight teeth.

Charlie noticed a slight accent. "Where are you from, Bella?"

"Puerto Rico, have you ever been there?" She leaned forward, planting her chin in the palm of her left hand; her elbow resting on the table.

"No, maybe one day my wife and I will visit. I understand it's very beautiful." Charlie cleared his throat. "You don't have a very heavy accent."

Bella leaned back when Charlie mentioned his wife. "Yes, my country is very beautiful. My father was an American. English is my first language. After he died, my mother only spoke Spanish."

"I'm sorry for your loss." Charlie's firm expression softened.

She shook her head. "It was a long time ago."

Charlie thought it was odd that he didn't see any sadness in Bella when she mentioned her dead father. *I wonder if she is looking for a father figure.* He decided not to go down that rabbit hole just now and continued with her interview. "When you say that you cleaned the cabin, what exactly did you do?"

"What I do every night in every cabin. I straighten things up, dust, vacuum, clean the bathroom, and replace the linens. The last thing I do is turn down the bed and put chocolate mints on the pillows."

"Did you go back into their cabin after you cleaned?"

Bella straightened, crossing her arms over her bounteous chest. "No, I do my job well, no reason to go back into their cabin."

"There's no reason to be defensive, Bella. Detective McClung is not questioning your efficiency."

Her posture relaxed. "May I have more coffee?"

"Help yourself." Charlie wanted more coffee but waited for Bella to be seated.

Bella pulled her chair close to the table and then dipped a lemon biscotti into her coffee as she watched Charlie pour coffee into his cup and Officer Watson's. "I would have done that if you had asked."

"That's not your job to wait on us." Charlie saw her constant smile dip into a frown, just for a moment. "Did you happen to see either one of the Fergusons later that night, after you had cleaned their room, maybe just in passing?"

"No," Bella immediately clipped the question.

Charlie chuckled, "You seem pretty confident in that."

Her eyes cut quickly to Officer Watson. "Yes, I am."

"Hmm, that's strange because Peter Ferguson stated that you approached him in the Stargazer lounge that night." Charlie flipped pages of the notepad, finding the correct page, he said, "Yep, that's what he said." He looked at Bella. "How do you explain that? Is he mistaken?"

She continued to smile, "Well, then, let me think. Oh, yes, I do remember I ran into him one night at the Stargazer, but I don't recall it being the night his wife died." Bella tilted her head, "Maybe it was that night," and then shrugged with a little giggle.

Charlie wasn't going to let her sweet innocent face change his direction of inquiry. "Why were you in the Stargazer lounge? Did you know he was going to be there?"

"You act as if it was some sinister plot, a clandestine rendezvous." Bella sipped her coffee. "It was nothing of the sort."

Her finger rubbed the handle of the cup and with a sly grin she almost purred, "I told you I'm good at what I do."

She took another sip, fluttering her eyelashes as she watched both men watch her. After setting down the cup, Bella smoothed away invisible crumbs from her chest, while she continued with her explanation, "I finished cleaning my assigned cabins, was bored, so I went to the bar and asked if I could help."

"Out of all of the bars onboard, why that one?"

"Because of the tips. It's the most crowded bar onboard." She snorted, "I'm not going to work for nothing."

Charlie smirked. "So, just a happy accident you ran into him there?"

"Mhm, that's right, just a happy accident."

"What time did you just happen to run into Peter at the bar?"

Bella tapped her finger against her cheek as she stared at the buffet. "Hmm, I don't know, ten o'clock, maybe."

Charlie wrote down the time and then decided to shift his line of questioning. "Are you married or have a boyfriend, someone special in your life?"

"Why is that any of your business?" Bella's smile disappeared.

Officer Watson rapped the table with three of his fingers. "Because this is a murder investigation and because Detective McClung asked you and you will answer it, now." He was growing impatient with her cuteness.

"Murder! You think she was murdered and I have something to do with it." Bella appeared to be shocked.

Officer Watson threw up his hands. "Don't bloody toy with us. You said you knew why you were here. Answer the question, girl."

Charlie almost laughed. He liked this side of Watson. *So were going to play good cop, bad cop. Let's see how this plays out.* He sat back and watched.

Bella was silent.

"I order you to answer the question." Officer Watson glared at her. "Now."

Charlie could have sworn he saw Bella's ears pull back as she smiled sarcastically.

"I've never been married and I'm not involved with anyone. There! I've answered your question. May I leave now?"

Officer Watson smiled. "Thank you and no, you may not leave. I will tell you when you may go. Is that understood?"

"Yes, sir." Bella resumed her smile as she crumbled the partially eaten scone into tiny bits.

"Detective McClung, do you have any more questions?"

"Yes, I do. Bella, you have been seen, and quite a lot I may add, hanging around Peter Ferguson. Why is that?"

She shrugged, "He's nice to me."

"I don't understand. Aren't most people nice to you? I mean, I know my wife and I are. Was Tammy mean to you? Why is Peter so special?" Charlie wasn't going to settle for her vanilla answer.

Bella wiped her hands together, dusting crumbs from them onto the saucer that contained the remains of the destroyed scone. "Yes, everyone is nice to me. Mrs. Ferguson wasn't mean but she seemed to just tolerate me. And don't ask me why. It was just a feeling."

Charlie spoke softly, "But why dote on Peter? Tell me what is so special about him? Can you do that, Bella?"

She bit her bottom lip and stared at her lap. "I watch how he treats his wife." Bella looked up. "He's kind to her and she doesn't seem to notice. I think he deserves better."

"Meaning you?"

Bella straightened her shoulders, holding her head high. "Yes, why not me? I can appreciate a good man."

Charlie squinted, "But I still don't understand why you chose Peter. I mean, don't I treat my wife like a queen?"

"Yes."

"So, why not me?"

Bella grinned, "Because your wife adores you."

Charlie looked directly into her eyes. "So because she didn't display enough affection toward her husband, she didn't deserve him. Is that what you're saying?"

"That sounds so callous but yes, I guess so. I would have made him a better wife."

Charlie tugged his earlobe. "Did you ever think she was a private person? That maybe behind closed doors she may have been more affectionate?"

Bella stared at a spot on the wall, between the two men. "No, she wasn't."

"But how do you know that, Bella."

Her eyes shot toward Charlie. "Because I know. I've seen women like her before. Peter was nice to me." Bella patted her hand softly on her chest.

"I give up." Charlie pushed away from the table. "Bella, did you kill Tammy to get her out of the way so you could have Peter all to yourself."

Bella laughed. "No, I didn't kill Tammy. Maybe she killed herself. Have you thought about that?"

Charlie shook his head. "No, why would she do that? Do you know something we don't know?"

She leaned forward and stabbed the table with her index finger. "Maybe this whole renewal ceremony was just a way to convince herself that Peter still belonged to her. But once she saw me and how Peter looked at me, she realized the truth and couldn't stand the fact that he fancied someone else." Bella jabbed the table with her finger again. "Me!"

"Well, I must say, that's some imagination. I think you may be a tiny bit deluded and enamored with yourself, because Peter told us," Charlie motioned between himself and Watson and then ran his finger down the pages of the notepad, "that their marriage was solid, they were best friends, truly loved each other, and Tammy was his world."

Charlie looked at Bella. He could almost feel the heat from the anger seething from inside of her. "He also said any other women were just passing fancies."

Bella's green eyes sparked with fury, inhaling deeply through her nose, she then breathed softly and smiled.

Charlie watched her face transform from enraged demon to serene angel. *This is one dangerous female.*

"And still you don't understand, but then again, you are *just* a man." Smiling, Bella bit her bottom lip. "I had nothing to do with whatever you think happened. May I please go back to work?"

Officer Watson looked to Charlie, who nodded. "You may leave." He flicked his hand toward the door.

Bella sashayed to the door, turned, winked at them, and then pushed open the door.

Chapter 13

Marian slipped into the interview room. "Man, I don't ever want to be on her bad side. She's a wee bit scary. We'll have to remember to tip her well before we disembark."

"You heard all of it?" Charlie rubbed the back of his neck to ease the tension.

"Yes." She stood behind her husband and rubbed the tight muscles in his shoulders.

"I didn't even notice you open the door, Mrs. McClung, I mean Marian. You're quite good at eavesdropping."

Charlie moaned, "I didn't realize that I married a sneak."

Marian jerked her hands away from him.

"Hey, don't stop. That's a compliment in my eyes. That trait can come in very handy." Charlie reached over his shoulder, grabbed her hand, kissed it, and then placed it back on his shoulder. "Keep doing your magic."

Marian kneaded his shoulders. "How many more are you going to interview today?"

"Only one more, Sophia Jackson. The other three will have to wait." Officer Watson stood and stretched his six-foot-five-inch frame. "May I get you a cup of tea, Marian?"

Marian patted her hands on Charlie's biceps. "No, thanks. I've got to run to the ladies room before Sophia arrives." She paused at the door. "You don't really think she has anything to do with Tammy's death, do you? Sophia, I mean."

Charlie tilted his head side-to-side, stretching his neck muscles. "Who knows? Just on gut instinct? No, I don't. But I've been surprised before." He shook his head as he remembered back to just two weeks ago.

Marian saw the sadness on Charlie's face, knowing it was Josephine he was thinking about. She blew him a kiss and was out the door.

Charlie pulled up a chair and got ready for the next interview. Before he could settle in, the conference room door flew open without warning.

"Hello, gentleman. I hope this won't take long. I've got early dinner plans and it takes me at least an hour to get gorgeous." Sophia's long blonde hair fluttered behind her as she breezed into the room. She hiked up her peasant skirt as she sat down and crossed her long tanned legs.

Charlie barely had time to stand before she sat across from him. "No."

"All right then, I'm ready. Fire away with your first question."

Flipping the notepad to a blank page, Charlie began. "When did you first meet Peter Ferguson?"

Sophia answered quickly, "Three years ago when I went to work for a medical device company. He's the regional manager of my territory."

"What's your territory?"

"Part of the southern district, Georgia."

Charlie paused as a question popped into his head. "Just Georgia? Ever go to Puerto Rico?"

"No, only Georgia, but Peter's territory covers Puerto Rico. He goes there all the time."

Charlie nodded slightly, "Hmm, have you ever gone there with him?"

"No, but," Sophia grinned, "I'm hoping to get assigned there one day. Now that I'm single, I'd love to move there." Her leg began to swing. "Man, that would be like working in heaven."

"Do you know if Tammy ever went with him to Puerto Rico?"

She scrunched up her face and shoulders, "Maybe once or twice in the three years that I've been working there. Now, if I were his wife, he'd never leave me behind. No, sir."

"Did Peter not want her to go?" Charlie wondered if it had anything to do with Bella.

"I don't think so."

Charlie stood, walked to the buffet, retrieved a tray with a pitcher of lemon water and few glasses, and then returned to the table. "So why do you think Tammy didn't go? Did she have a job?" He offered Sophia a glass of water.

"No, she didn't work but I know she did volunteer work somewhere, maybe a children's hospital." She accepted the glass and took a sip of water.

"I'm going to be blunt with this next question. Are you and Peter involved?"

Sophia laughed, "God, no. He's practically old enough to be my father. He's great to have fun with but sexually, no way." Her back stiffened and her laughter died suddenly. "Did he tell you we're having an affair?"

"No, he said it was strictly a work relationship."

"Whew, I love my job. I'd hate to have to quit because of his misconstrued ideas about us."

Charlie wet his dry mouth, and then continued, "Do you know of any affairs he may have had or is currently having?"

She shook her head. "Not one specific person, but rumor is that he likes women and Tammy didn't seem to care. Go figure." Sophia ran her fingers around the sweating glass.

"I see. But he's never tried to start anything with you?" Charlie really wanted to wrap up the interview.

"Never... " Sophia paused, "but last night he did appear to be jealous because I was flirting with that fine first officer, Jameson." She looked at Officer Watson. "Tell that sexy beast I'll meet him anytime and anywhere."

Officer Watson's deadpan expression didn't flinch. "Yes, ma'am, I will pass on your message."

"Thank you!"

"I have one or two more questions, then I think we're finished." Charlie sighed heavily. "Do you know of anyone who would want to harm Tammy?"

"If you're asking if I think Peter would, that answer is a flat out no and I don't know of anyone else who would want to either." Sophia tucked a few strands of fine blonde hair behind her ears.

Charlie closed his notepad. "Last question, did Peter ever mention any allergies that Tammy had?"

Sophia laughed, "Yeah, whenever he ate seafood or anything with peanuts, he'd brush his teeth afterward. He said Tammy was overly paranoid about her so-called allergies. I asked him once why he called them her so-called allergies, and he said he'd never seen any kind of reaction to either one but he played along with Tammy to make her happy."

"One last question, promise, this is the last one, when did you decide to join Jack on this cruise?"

Sophia smirked. "Two weeks ago, when his darling wife announced she was leaving him."

"That's brutal. Poor, Jack, I didn't know the wound was so fresh."

"Yeah, at least I gave my husband fair warning. I told him a year ago that things had to change or I'd be history."

"I'd say that was fair. Sorry, but one more question, when did you know that Peter would be on this cruise?"

"When I saw him at the poolside bar yesterday."

Charlie stood and extended his hand toward Sophia. "That's all for now. Thank you for your time. I hope you still have time to get gorgeous."

"I've got plenty of time, besides it doesn't hurt to make a man wait, builds up their anticipation if you know what I mean." Sophia flipped her long tresses behind her shoulders as she strutted out of the room.

Marian entered the room. "That didn't take too long."

Both men stood and stretched.

"I wondered if Sophia has always been a tease or if this is a new development now that she's divorced." Marian walked behind Charlie, wrapping her arms around his waist and squeezing him.

Officer Watson gathered his legal pad and fountain pen. "Since we finished this one early enough to delay the next ones, I'll have messages sent to Henry, Antonio, and Kaye Tolbert."

"I don't want to wait too long." Charlie turned and cupped Marian's chin. "Would you mind if we finished them tonight?"

"Of course not, this is fun." Marian stood tip-toed and kissed his cheek.

"What do you say, Watson? Are you up for it?"

Officer Watson massaged his right elbow. "I would like to put this to bed as soon as possible. Henry and Antonio will not be a problem but Mrs. Tolbert could be since she's a passenger and not an employee."

Charlie squeezed the back of his neck. Marian forced him to sit down and began to knead the muscles for him. She asked, "What time was Mrs. Tolbert supposed to be here?"

"I'm here now. I hope it's not a problem." The stately woman strode into the room, her jet black hair cut into a blunt bob, seemed to cradle her head like a stocking cap. "I have something more important to do during the time that was given to me. The interview must be now." Kaye Tolbert stared at the men, daring them to defy her.

Marian patted Charlie's back and left the room, feeling invisible.

Officer Watson and Charlie returned her glare.

"Well, gentlemen?"

Charlie motioned for her to take a seat. Officer Watson turned and made his way to the wall phone.

"Would you like something to eat or drink while we wait for Officer Watson to return?"

"No, thank you," Kaye Tolbert looked at her watch and then rolled her eyes.

Charlie studied the uptight woman as they waited for Watson to finish giving instructions to the person on the other end. *I wonder if she's always this unpleasant or if she's trying to cover up her anxieties about her interview.*

Watson sat down. "I am Officer Phillip Watson and this is Detective Charlie McClung. We are interviewing guests and employees who have come in contact with Peter and Tammy Ferguson."

"I know who you are and why I am here. Can you just ask me whatever you want to know?" Kaye Tolbert crossed her arms, drumming her fingers on her bicep.

Charlie really didn't like this woman and wanted this interview to end sooner than she did. "Tammy Ferguson was murdered. You were seen arguing with her husband last night. Can you explain?"

"My discussion with Mr. Ferguson is our business, none of your concern. Next question."

Under the table, Charlie balled his hands into fists. "We will ask Peter Ferguson who is very forthcoming and willing to cooperate to help solve the murder of his wife."

"That was a statement, not a question. Do you have any other questions or am I free to go?" She started to rise.

Charlie slammed his fist on the table, thinking, *two can play this game of hardball.* "Look, from where I sit, you look like the perfect suspect for the murder of Tammy Ferguson. Now, why should I not think otherwise? You are not cooperating and you were seen arguing with the victim's husband. Are you having an affair with him? Were you angry with him because he was with a more attractive, younger woman instead of you last night?"

She gritted her teeth. "How dare you accuse me of having an affair? I'm a married woman and I'll not have you sullying my reputation!"

"Then answer my question. Why were you arguing with Peter Ferguson?"

Kaye Tolbert sat like an Easter Island monolith.

Charlie bounced the end of his pen against the notepad, wondering if he should wait her out or keep pounding at her. *Pound away!* "Are you protecting him? Or are you afraid you'll slip up and incriminate yourself? Which is it, Kaye Tolbert? Protecting your lover or yourself?"

She considered his questions and calmly replied, "You apparently have a problem with your short-term memory. Maybe you should consider writing down my answers. I am not nor have I ever had an affair with Peter Ferguson."

"No, I think you have the problem. You never answered my question. You only warned me not to … how did you phrase it … sully your reputation. You didn't confirm nor actually deny an affair."

"Any intelligent human would have understood my statement."

Charlie snorted. "Was that man sitting across from you at the Captain's dinner your husband?"

"Yes."

"Does he know about your relationship with Peter Ferguson? Maybe we should question him. What do you think Watson?"

Her eyes widened slightly and her nostrils flared.

Officer Watson stood. "I think I'll give your cabin a ring or have one of my men collect him for an interview."

"No, wait." She licked her dry lips, eyes darting to the lemon water.

I've got her now, Charlie celebrated silently. "Would you like some water?"

She was almost docile as she nodded, "Please."

Charlie slid the glass within her reach. "Now, what is your relationship with Peter Ferguson?"

"I'm his sponsor," she mumbled into the water.

"I'm sorry. Did you say his sponsor?" Officer Watson gawked at the shapely woman and thought about Peter's soft belly. "As in overeaters?"

Charlie corrected Watson, "Alcoholic Anonymous and your husband doesn't know, does he?"

Kaye Tolbert shook her head. "He never even knew I had a problem." She looked at them with glassy brown eyes. "Please don't tell him, please."

"How long sober?" Charlie's voice was softer, more caring.

"Almost two years." Kaye smiled, proud of her accomplishment.

Charlie smiled with her. "Congratulations. So you must have been arguing about Peter's drinking. How long has he been attending meetings?"

"Not long, only two months." She smirked, "I was a sponsor for the first time and I failed."

Reaching across the narrow table, Charlie patted her hand, recently manicured. "Don't give up on him. He's going through a rough patch, encourage him, maybe he'll come around."

Kaye was surprised at Charlie's tenderness toward her after she had been such a horrible bitch. "I'm sorry for my attitude. I don't want anyone to know that I'm a recovering alcoholic. It makes me feel weak and inferior, so I put on an air of strength." She gave a weak laugh. "I guess I'm too over-the-top."

Charlie held up his index finger and thumb about an inch apart. "I'd say a wee bit."

"I really would like to help solve your mystery but I really don't know anything. Peter and I met when he joined the group. I met Tammy for the first time at their renewal ceremony. She thought I knew Peter through work, so did my husband."

"Where do you work?"

"I'm a vice president of a bank."

Charlie pushed back his chair and stood up. "I think we're finished. And if Peter does anything, says anything that sounds suspicious, please be sure and let us know. Thank you for your time, Mrs. Tolbert."

She shook his hand. "I wish I could help."

Chapter 14

"Holy crap!" Jack Jackson jerked his head away from the microscope and immediately returned his eyes, just to verify what he saw.

Doctor Nelson trotted to his side. "What is it, Jack? What did you find?"

"Doc, you've got to see for yourself."

Doctor Nelson adjusted the objective lenses and fine focus. "Is this a prank, Jack?" He studied the younger man's face. "You're serious."

Jack nodded.

Doctor Nelson looked at the object again. "But it can't be. How…?"

"We've got to tell McClung and Watson. They should be in the interview room. I've got to stop by the photoshop first. I took pictures of it. Got to prove it to them. They won't believe it unless they see it."

♣

Charlie looked out into the hallway. Marian was speaking in hushed tones with Jack. "Hey! Are you two plotting on me?"

Marian ran to her husband's side, grabbing his arm, pulling him back into the interview room. "Oh, this is unbelievable; you and Watson have got to hear what Jack has found."

"What? Tell me."

"Jack's got to explain this, it's too bizarre. Only he can do it justice."

Jack Jackson was rubbing his hands together. "This is a first for me, McClung, and it's so far out there, I can barely believe it myself."

Officer Watson was on the phone when they re-entered the room.

"Watson, we're not finished. Jack has found something concerning Tammy's death. Evidently, it's a whopper!"

"Oh, is that right? Well, I best sit down for this."

Jack went straight to the buffet and poured a cup of coffee. "You should all sit down. This is a marvelous find."

"You have our undivided attention, stop being so dramatic and tell us what you've found." Charlie wanted to be alone with Marian and forget about murder, statements, and evidence.

Jack turned around a chair, straddled it, and then hung his arms over the back and drank his coffee. "You remember the puncture wounds in her gums? And do you remember the brown flake-like things in Tammy's toothbrush? We thought it was trail mix."

"Yes," they all agreed.

"Well, it was trail mix, and I'm glad it was there because if it hadn't been, I probably wouldn't have examined the toothbrush as closely as I did under the microscope. A lesson learned there." Jack paused and looked around at each of their faces. "You're going to have a hard time believing this. Guess what I found embedded in the bristles … bee stingers."

"Ah, don't be a cheeky monkey," Watson groaned. "I'm too tired to be playing games."

"No, I'm serious. Bee stingers. Five honey bee stingers to be exact." He reached underneath his white lab coat and pulled out a large envelope that was tucked in the back of his pants, tossing it on the table. "I've got pictures to prove it."

Sure enough, there were four pictures of the toothbrush and a picture of the five stingers, side by side with their venom sacs clearly attached. He had included the previous picture of Tammy's gums and two new ones as well.

Charlie studied the pictures before passing them on to Watson. "That's a fret, now." He shook his head and grinned. "Just when you think you've heard everything."

"Are you telling us that Mrs. Ferguson was stung to death?" Officer Watson pulled his head back in disbelief.

"In a weird way, but yes, she must have been highly allergic to bees. It's an ingenious way to commit murder."

"Like my father but more so. I mean allergic to bees, not murdered," Marian looked at Charlie. "Did Peter tell any of you that Tammy was allergic to bees?"

Charlie tugged his ear, "No. He only mentioned peanuts and shellfish and only mildly allergic to those."

"Strange, don't you think?" Jack jumped up to refill his cup. "This is the last of the coffee. Anyone else want it?"

"No, but I'll have some tea." After making a cup of tea, Marian leaned against the buffet and sipped quietly. "Peter may not have mentioned it because you don't have bees at sea."

"So, Jack, explain to us what you think happened." Charlie joined his wife and shared her cup of tea.

"We can now rule out any suspects who didn't have access to the Ferguson's cabin because someone carefully and skillfully hid the stingers in Tammy's toothbrush. The killer must have placed stingers on either side of the brush to make sure at least one of them would penetrate her gums."

Charlie put his fists on his hips and began to pace. "But do you know how long the stingers have been in the brush? Could they have been in it for a few days and just now worked their way out enough to sting her?"

"Anything is possible but if someone was trying to kill her, I don't think they would have taken the chance, crossed their fingers, and hoped the stingers would work their way out and inject their poison. To double-check my theory, I re-examined the body an hour or so ago and sure enough, embedded under the gum line, at the very back of her mouth are two more stingers. If she was highly allergic to the bee venom, it would have been enough to send her into shock."

Marian filled her cup and then handed it to Charlie. "You're right, but who knew she was allergic to bees? Surely Peter had to know." Charlie drank the hot tea, hoping it would soothe the tension in his stomach.

"I'll arrange another interview with Mr. Ferguson." Officer Watson made the phone call straight away and returned to the table. "All right then, I asked for him to meet us tomorrow after we leave port."

Charlie sighed heavily. "Henry and Antonio, when are they scheduled?"

"Tonight, after eight o'clock but if you wish, they can easily be rearranged."

Charlie draped his arm across Marian's shoulders. "I would like both of them put off until tomorrow. This is my honeymoon and I'd like to spend the rest of the night with my wife." He kissed her temple. "I don't think they'll jump ship. One more day can't possibly make a difference."

"Sounds splendid. I've paperwork to catch up on tonight." Officer Watson smiled, "No worries, I'll take care of it and leave you a message. Go enjoy the rest of the day. Like you said, no one's going anywhere."

Chapter 15

Charlie and Marian sat in an open-air café watching dozens of tourists, just like themselves, pass by. Charlie enjoyed watching Marian sip a beer from a frosty mug. He never understood the appeal of margaritas and daiquiris and was pleasantly surprised to find that his gentle bride felt the same way.

"Mmm, nothing like an ice cold beer on a hot day." Charlie held up his mug and drank.

Marian grinned, "You can't beat it. I'm glad we found this spot. It's perfect for spying." She pointed her head toward the street.

Her eyes were hidden behind her black sunglasses but Charlie spotted who had caught Marian's attention.

Bella walked with Peter Ferguson. He didn't seem to mind that she was hanging onto his arm as she pointed to cheap trinkets that a sidewalk vendor had for sale. He seemed to enjoy it a bit too much considering his wife, supposedly his world, had just died.

"He's definitely breezed through the five stages of grief in a matter of days and has apparently moved on with his life," Charlie frowned. "Peter must not have ever truly loved Tammy to so casually replace her."

"Nope."

Even though Marian's eyes were hidden behind the dark sunglasses, Charlie knew they were glassy as she was probably thinking about Lee's death. Even though her husband had been dead for eleven years, she had a hard time letting go. But with every smile, every touch, each breath Marian took, he could feel her love for him. Charlie knew her heart now belonged to him.

Gazing at Marian, Charlie remembered when he first met her, just over three months ago. Her beauty attracted him initially but it was Marian's soul that stunned him. The roots of his love for her grew deeper with each passing moment. His heart ached as he thought of how close he had come to losing her, twice. Nothing could sever his love for her, not even death. Turning his attention back to the crowded street, Charlie took a long sip of beer, hoping to wash away the feeling of dreadful loss.

"Look, Marian," Charlie said softly. "Do you see who's trailing Peter and Bella?"

She searched the crowd for a familiar face and found one, Henry. "Well, well, this is getting pretty interesting, wouldn't you say?"

Charlie watched the couple saunter carefree down the sidewalk, oblivious to their stalker. "Henry's pretty good at tailing. He must've done it before." He watched as Henry strategically hid behind colorful sarapes hanging high, enabling him to peek without being seen by Peter and Bella.

"Kind of makes one feel like God, watching people without them realizing they are being watched." Marian looked around the café. "I wonder if anyone is watching us, besides God I mean?"

"Don't worry, we're not doing anything to interest anyone, and besides, I'll protect you from any evildoers." Charlie grinned, "Trust me?"

Marian sat down the sweaty mug, resting her elbows on the table, she put her chin onto the palms of her hands. "How could I ever not trust you? I'm living proof."

He grabbed her wrists, pulled her closer, and then kissed her nose. "I don't like to be reminded."

"Mmm, I love you, Charlie." Marian leaned across the table, captured his head between her hands, and then kissed him deeply. When she broke the kiss, Marian sat back with a smug grin. "Can I ask you a question?"

"Is it, will you take me back to our cabin?"

She giggled, "Not a bad idea but no that's not the question. My question is, are we going to stalk the stalker who's stalking Peter and Bella?"

"That's a lot of stalking. Going back to the cabin sounds like more fun to me." Charlie saw Henry slip out of view. "But yes, we are."

Marian drained her mug. "Let's go." She picked up a floppy straw hat that Charlie had bought earlier to keep the sun from burning her nose. "This should help keep my face hidden." Marian pulled it low, covering her forehead, "What do you think?"

"Can you see where you're going or am I to lead you around like you're blind?" Charlie adjusted her hat. "That's better." He put on his non-descript tan ball cap. "All right Mata Hari, let's get to stalking."

They strolled down the busy sidewalk just within sight of Henry, stopping whenever he stopped. Peter and Bella were out of their line of sight.

After about fifteen minutes of mindlessly browsing, Henry stood inside a doorway of an empty building, partially hidden by a street vendor's rack of braided bracelets. He kept his eye on a large gift shop sporting a sign advertising a courtyard restaurant inside.

"Do you think Peter and Bella are inside that shop?" Marian whispered. She and Charlie were on the opposite side of the street, eating snow cones as they stood in the shade of a clump of spindly trees.

Charlie grimaced in pain.

"Brain freeze?"

He nodded. After a few moments, Charlie moaned, "When will I ever learn?"

Marian whispered, "You're forty-seven, so I'd say never."

"I don't think you have to whisper. I can barely hear you. Henry certainly can't."

"I can't help it. Spying seems to call for whispering." Marian's voice was at a normal level.

Henry's head swiveled in their direction. Charlie turned his back and stepped in front of Marian.

"Do you think he heard us?"

"No, but I don't want him to spot us and to answer your earlier question, yes, I think they're in that shop, most likely at the restaurant inside." Charlie glanced over his shoulder.

Henry was going inside.

Marian gasped, "You don't think he's going to confront them, do you?"

Charlie tossed the empty paper cone into the trash. "Who knows? Follow me." He held her hand as they crossed the street.

They walked halfway by the large storefront window, stopping in front of a display of a giant suit of armor. "I can't see anything without being obvious. We're going in." Charlie walked back to the entrance Henry had used, looked at Marian, and said, "Ready?"

She grinned, "My heart's pounding but I'm ready."

The cold air blasted them as they stepped inside. Charlie searched the shelves for a glimpse of Henry. A flash of shiny black hair caught his eye from one of the side rooms.

Charlie poked Marian, who was admiring a pair of silver earrings. He pointed toward the room. They strolled in, looking up and down the room but Henry was gone. The room had two entrances.

"He must have doubled back on us." Charlie walked to the other entrance and motioned Marian to his side. "Look. He's heading toward the restaurant."

"What are we going to do?"

"Are you up for another beer?"

Marian nodded.

"Okay, let's walk to the bar carefree and casual and sit where we can see but not be seen."

Marian held up her thumb.

When they reached the door, Henry was standing there with one hand in his pants pocket. He was searching the small crowded open-air patio restaurant and didn't notice Charlie and Marian.

Marian held onto Charlie's arm. "What should we do now? Leave?"

"No, continue with our plan. But I'm going to speak with him first. I want to know why he's here." Charlie pushed through the glass door, walked up a little behind Henry, stood silently, and then scanned the patio. Peter and Bella were tucked away at a table for two shaded by a clump of tall banana trees.

"Well, Henry, escape from the boat?" Charlie extended his hand.

Henry flinched at the sound of Charlie's voice, unaware he was standing beside him. "Mr. McClung, you startled me. I am so sorry. I did not see you." Henry removed his hand from his pocket to shake hands with Charlie.

"I hear this is the place to be. Care to join us?"

Henry glanced toward Peter and Bella. "Yes, this place is the best. I was looking for a waiter friend of mine but I do not see him."

Marian smiled sweetly and lightly touched his shoulder, "Oh, Henry, please join us. Please."

Charlie stifled a chuckle behind his hand when he saw Marian flutter her lashes at Henry.

"You must, Henry. I insist! You've been very good to us. Let me buy you a beer. You're off duty right?" Charlie clamped Henry's shoulder and then walked him toward the far end of the bar.

Charlie and Marian sat together closest to the wall, forcing Henry's attention solely on them and away from Peter and Bella.

"So, Henry, what will you have?" Charlie greeted the bartender, "My wife will have a Corona in a frosty mug and the same for me. Henry?"

Henry glanced over his shoulder to make sure his quarry was still cornered. "Just a Coke, thank you." He looked at Charlie, "I am technically always on duty."

Charlie had a perfect line of sight to Peter and Bella, who had no clue they were even being watched. Marian held Henry's attention with her multitude of questions while Charlie watched Peter and Bella play cat and mouse. But Charlie was having a hard time solving the problem of who was the cat and who was the mouse.

"Isn't that amazing, Charlie?" Marian squeezed his forearm, "Henry and Bella knew each before they started working for the cruise line."

Damn, I should have been listening, Charlie cursed himself. "Well, they say, it's a small world." He turned most of his attention to Henry. "How did you two go about working for the same company?"

"I went to work for them straight out of high school, two years before Bella. On my first visit home, I ran into Bella. I guess she liked my stories of sea life and decided to work for them, too."

Loud melodious laughter floated over the tinkling music of the xylophone being played in the courtyard by a father-daughter duet.

Charlie glanced toward Bella who was holding her belly with one hand and wiping away tears of laughter with the other. Peter seemed pleased with his wit. Henry's lip was slightly curled in a snarl and he rose from the barstool.

"No, Henry, don't leave we were just getting to know you," Marian pouted.

Henry bowed slightly. "Thank you, madam, sir, for your kindness but I must be returning to the ship."

"Thank you, Henry, for making our trip such a pleasure. Your service is beyond exceptional." Charlie extended his hand.

Henry's smile was strained although he seemed pleased with Charlie's praise. "Again, thank you, I am happy you are satisfied." With another bow, he left without another look at Peter and Bella.

"Hmm, well, at least we, rather you, gathered some useful information." Charlie gave Marian a quick, one-armed hug. "I was too busy watching Peter play footsy with Bella. What else did you learn besides Bella and Henry both lived in Puerto Rico?"

"Not much more. Their mothers were friends, worked at the same restaurant. That's how they met. He likes his job and that's about it."

"We'll find out more after we question him." Charlie finished his beer. "Would you like another one?"

"No, I'm ready to head back to the ship. Looks like Peter and Bella are about to leave."

Peter motioned his waiter over and handed him what appeared to be a one hundred dollar bill, telling the grinning man to keep the change. Bella threaded her arm around Peter's and leaned her head against his shoulder as the two ambled out of the restaurant.

"Might as well follow them." Charlie grabbed Marian by her waist, helping her off the tall barstool.

As they walked out of the gift shop, Marian thought she saw someone duck behind a display of piñatas. The person was too short to be Henry. She passed it off as her imagination and one too many beers.

They followed Peter and Bella, watching them stroll in and out of gift shops. It appeared Peter was being very generous with his money. Each time they exited a shop, he was carrying one more bag and Bella was wearing a smug grin on her face.

They were almost to the gangway entrance when Henry swung behind Peter and Bella. He approached them with a gregarious smile and offered to carry Peter's bags who was more than happy to relinquish his burdens. Bella, on the other hand, didn't seem to be as happy to see Henry as Peter. She positioned herself so Peter would be in the middle of the trio.

"Peter is oblivious to the tension between Henry and Bella." Charlie squeezed Marian's hand.

She lightly scratched Charlie's back as they walked down the pier. "Maybe he doesn't care. I mean, he'll probably never see the two of them again. He can't possibly be serious about Bella."

"You never know. Maybe the two of them are in cahoots. You know, knock off the old and bring in the new."

"That's a rather harsh way to put it but then again, it may be exactly what happened." Marian watched the three people in front of her. "I don't know. Peter just doesn't look like the criminal kind."

"They rarely do. That's what makes them so dangerous."

At the gangway, Bella and Henry split off from Peter. They went up the crew gangway while Peter strolled up the one designated for guests. Charlie and Marian lingered behind until the three disappeared inside the hull.

Marian looked over her shoulder. "Charlie, I think someone is following us, look." She pointed toward the ship's hospitality tent.

"I don't see anything but we'll keep our eyes open." He kissed her temple. "Hopefully, it's nothing to be concerned about."

Marian looked again, seeing nothing suspicious. "Yeah, I guess all of this espionage is making my imagination run wild."

Chapter 16

"What do you think you are doing? Hmm? Do you think he's going to marry you? Do you?"

Bella rolled her eyes and laughed, "Henry, I don't care if he marries me or not. I'm trying to get all I can from him." She turned her back on him, pulled some towels from the shelf, and then loaded the pile onto her cart. "I'm not stupid. He's a user, a taker."

"So what does that make you, huh?" Henry grabbed her shoulders.

She jerked away. "I'm a grown woman. I'll do what I want." Bella pushed the cart out of the linen room.

"Be careful Bella. He's not what you think."

Bella studied Henry's face and wondered why she couldn't love him. He was handsome enough, a skillful lover. She tried to pretend but… Bella shook her head, *maybe I'm not capable of loving.* "Henry, I know what I'm doing. I know his kind too well."

Henry held onto her cart. "Yeah, I bet that's what your mother thought, too, and look what that got her."

She gritted her teeth. "You leave my mama out of this. This has nothing to do with her, besides you're one to be talking." Bella shoved the cart, running over Henry's foot. "I've got cabins to turn down."

Henry watched her disappear around the corner. He raised his fist to hit the wall, but instead, pounded it against his open palm. He took a deep breath and smoothed back his hair, making sure every strand was in place. Glancing at his watch, he decided he had just enough time to deliver all of the afternoon canapés to the suites and refill their ice buckets before going to the conference room to be interviewed.

Henry wondered why they were making such a fuss over one dead woman who died from anaphylactic shock. *She should have been more careful what she put into her mouth, maybe then, she wouldn't have died.* He decided that he had more important things to worry about, namely, Bella. How was he going to keep her from getting into more trouble?

Chapter 17

"Charlie, what do you think of us having dinner in our cabin? We can order room service and a bottle of wine, be alone ..." Marian ran her fingers down his cheek as he lay on his back staring at the ceiling.

He held her hand and kissed each fingertip. "I think it's a brilliant idea." Charlie rolled onto his side, stared into her eyes, "Great minds think alike." He pushed her hair behind her ear. "It seems like our honeymoon is more like a circus. I know this isn't what you envisioned for us, is it?"

"Oh, no it's not a circus. Not at all. It's more like murder mystery dinner theater or the game of Clue." She smiled. "But it's okay. I'm with you. We're a team." Marian pushed herself up, leaned against the headboard, and patted her lap. "Come here. Let me smooth your furrowed brow."

Charlie obeyed and enjoyed her gentle touch as she massaged his temples.

"Look, I didn't go into this marriage with blinders on. You're a cop. I know what cops do. I'll support you and never make you feel guilty about doing your job. That is, as long as I'm number one, and you keep me informed. Deal?"

"Nothing will ever take your place as number one in my life. Your pedestal is too high and too strong to be conquered." Charlie rolled over to sit on the side of the bed. "I'll ring room service now. What would you like?"

Marian pressed against his bare back. His warmth felt good. Hanging her head over his shoulder, she sighed. "I don't know. We've dined like kings the past few days. I think I'd like something simple. What do you say?"

Charlie pulled her around to sit on his lap. "Well, Mrs. McClung, you shall have whatever your heart desires. Peanut butter and jelly sandwiches?"

Marian giggled. "No, not that simple. What about pizza or tacos or nachos?" She gasped with a surprised look on her face. "I know! We'll order nothing but appetizers and a pizza and beer."

"Sounds like a plan to me. Oh, we've got to have cookies, too." Charlie hugged Marian. "You're my kind of gal."

"Well, I think it's a bit late to decide otherwise. Maybe this will seal your decision." She kissed him, slow and deep, feeling his body responding, Marian broke the kiss.

"Woman, you're killing me." Charlie was thinking about the interviews he had to do in less than an hour. He needed to place their room service order but all he wanted to do was roll over in the bed with her.

Marian jumped up. "Am I too wicked?" She jumped away from his reach. "Remember what George Hamilton said."

In a Count Dracula voice, Charlie answered, "With you, never a quickie, always a longie." He rubbed his face with both hands and then shook his head. "Augh! I want this Ferguson thing to be over with."

Charlie held out his hand. "Come here." Marian accepted and sat on his lap. "Promise me a *longie*."

"Promise." She crossed her heart.

"Tonight."

"Double promise."

Charlie pushed her from his lap and then slapped her butt as she stood. "Get dressed. I've got interviews and you've got eavesdropping to do. I'll place our order." He picked up the phone, dialing he asked her, "Two of everything and a cheese pizza?"

From the closet, Marian yelled, "Yeah, and don't forget the beer and cookies."

Chapter 18

The conference room buffet looked naked compared to the other day's afternoon tea. Only two pitchers of water and a few glasses sat in the center of the large table. Charlie and Officer Watson paced around the room planning their interview strategy as they waited for Peter Ferguson to appear, the first of their three interviews.

"If you had to wager, who would you say killed Mrs. Ferguson?" Officer Watson stopped and stared out the window.

"That's a tough one. We know it had to be someone with access to the room after the Fergusons left their cabin for dinner."

"So you're ruling out the husband?"

Charlie shook his head. "No, he could've put the stingers in the toothbrush before he left for the bar or instructed someone else to do it."

"I suppose so. Either way, he's guilty." Officer Watson stared at the waves through the oversized window, a ship on the distant horizon.

"Yeah and get this, Marian and I saw Peter and Bella together on shore. And Henry was following them."

"You don't say. Hmm, that is interesting. How are you going to approach that line of questioning?"

Charlie grinned, "I'll point blank tell him I saw him and ask him to explain. I won't mention that Henry was following them. Henry will have to explain why."

"I like it, cut to the chase, and maybe we can get this solved sooner rather than later. He certainly can't deny they were together."

"Nope, we've got him red-handed. What I really want to know is how long they have really known each other. Bella lived in Puerto Rico where, according to Sophia, Peter visits quite often because of work."

Officer Watson bobbed his head. "Ah, I see. If there was a relationship between them before the cruise, then maybe this was just the right spot to dispose of the wife."

"Right, who else would know of her bee allergy besides the husband who in turn tells his mistress, Bella, who has access to the suite?"

"They may have gotten away with it too. They would never have considered the possibility of a medical examiner being on board to say it was anything other than an allergic reaction."

"Yep." Charlie glanced at his watch and then up to the clock above the door. Only a few more minutes to wait. He walked to a wall covered in portraits of the ship's past captains. "Do you know many of these men?"

Officer Watson joined Charlie. "A few of them." He pointed to the ones he knew. "I like my current captain the best. The man has a lively sense of humor. Every now and then, he'll bring his cat onboard. Dresses the cat in a little captain's uniform his wife made. Cap and all."

Charlie laughed. "I guess sea life can be monotonous. Need something to lighten it up."

Officer Watson agreed. "Oh, by the way, I checked on the Ferguson's booking. They booked two months ago. And I double-checked on Jackson's, too. He made his a month ago. His booking was changed two weeks ago from his wife to his sister."

"Nothing suspicious there, I guess."

"Nope."

"You know, I'm curious about this Antonio Caruso. Why was he in their suite? And why was she wearing those panties? According to Peter, Tammy wasn't expecting him. So who were they for?"

"You're thinking that maybe Tammy and Caruso were—"

Charlie cut off Watson, "That's exactly what I'm thinking."

"Well, that puts a twist in the ole knickers, no pun intended."

Charlie chuckled. "This Caruso fellow could have done it. He admits he was there. Motive? Maybe we'll find one when we question him."

Lacing his fingers, Watson cracked his knuckles, "Who knows what deep, dark, sordid secrets we'll discover once they begin to spill their guts?"

"Yeah, too early in the game to call."

The conference room door flung open. "Gentleman, I'm surprised I was summoned again. I hope you can make this quick. I've got plans that won't wait."

"Yes, I know Bella is on a schedule." Officer Watson poured a glass of water. "Would you like a glass? You look … what's that expression?" He looked at Charlie for the answer.

"Green around the gills? Is that the one you're looking for?"

Officer Watson swallowed a sip of water. "Ah, yes, that's the one. Mr. Ferguson, please take a seat." He sat a glass of water before Peter.

Peter Ferguson held the glass with both hands, hoping the chilled glass would keep him from sweating. "I'm not sure what you mean by that remark."

Charlie and Officer Watson rolled their eyes. Watson nodded, "McClung, will you clarify?"

"Does the restaurant, Inside Patio, mean anything to you?" Charlie watched as Peter's jaw tightened, his Adam's apple dipped, and his eyes widened. "It's not that hard of a question, Peter, either it does or it doesn't."

Peter's nose flared then he relaxed and smiled. "You know the answer to that question already."

"Yeah, but I'd kind of like to hear it from you. So Peter, tell me about the Inside Patio restaurant. Is it a cozy place?" Charlie enjoyed watching interviewees with a guilty conscience squirm. And this one was about to explode.

Peter pursed his lips.

Charlie grinned, knowing how much Peter probably hated him right now. "Ah, come on, Peter, are you at a loss for words?" He leaned in. "Well, I can describe what I saw if you like."

Peter sneered, "Yeah, tell me, oh great detective, what you saw. I want to see how brilliant you are."

Ah, the worm has turned, not so nice now. Charlie sat back, "Well, the missus and I ambled into the Inside Patio to have a cold beer. A very lovely place, I must say. The ambiance is very relaxing, one could say cozy, maybe even romantic in a way." He relished in Peter's obvious impatience. "Officer Watson, have you ever had the pleasure to dine there?"

"Why yes, I must agree with you, McClung, the ambiance is stunning and the food …" Watson made a drooling face, "is most spectacular. Pity you only had a beer. If you ever visit again, you must at least try their guacamole. The best I've ever eaten. Oh, and their—"

"Yeah, yeah, yeah, enough of the restaurant critique." Peter crossed his arms and scowled.

Charlie cleared his throat. "Yes, you're right. How rude of us. This meeting is all about you. We should be discussing you."

Tapping his chin with his index finger, Charlie looked up, trying to recollect his thoughts. "Let me see. Where was I? Oh, yes, well, low and behold, who did we see?"

"Entertain me, continue with your … musings."

"All right then. We saw you and Bella in a cozy little corner. It was as if the two of you were in your own little Shangri-La secluded from the rest of the world."

"Oh, that's lovely, McClung. You do have a way with words," Watson complimented.

"Thank you."

"For the love of God, will you please get to the point?" Peter huffed, turning red.

"If that's what you want?"

"Damn right! Just be out with it. Keep it short and simple!"

Charlie sat up straight. "Peter, we think you and Bella are having an affair. And we believe the affair started back in Puerto Rico. We know you travel there for work. And we know Bella lives there. Perhaps, Bella wanted more from you. Maybe she was tired of the scraps you were tossing her. So Bella killed your wife, who was in her way of having all of you to herself."

Peter clapped his hands. "Oh, you missed your calling, Detective McClung. Yeah, you should be writing fiction novels. You're wasting your talent just being a lowly cop." He drank the room temperature water sitting before him. "You have such a wild imagination. But you're wrong. First of all, I just met Bella. There's no way she's had time to develop deluded ideas about us. But continue with your fanciful tale, please. Tell me how she killed Tammy. Did Bella feed her a peanut?"

"I thought you said Tammy was mildly allergic to peanuts?"

Peter's hand froze mid-air. "Well, yeah. I was just being funny."

Charlie's face turned to stone. "So you think all of this is funny. You think your wife's murder, who you claimed was *your world*, is funny."

Peter fidgeted, "No, that's not what I meant. I uh …"

"Then what did you mean?" Charlie grabbed the edge of the table, thrusting his body forward.

"I don't know, uh, I guess, uh," Peter slid his chair back, stood and then began to pace. "I mean, how was Tammy killed?"

"Sit down, Mr. Ferguson," Officer Watson stood beside Peter until he sat.

"Let's see, Peter. You seem to think she died from anaphylactic shock. I mean you're the one who mentioned peanuts." Time was running short, Charlie knew Henry would arrive soon for his interview. He had to get to the point. "Was Tammy allergic to bees?"

"The doctor told me it was anaphylactic shock so why should I think otherwise?"

"I ask you again. Was Tammy allergic to bees?"

"Yes, yes, she was allergic to bees."

"Why did you fail to mention that when you were asked what she was allergic to?"

"Because we're in the middle of the freaking ocean! That's why! I thought it was something she had eaten. Whoever heard of bees being in the middle of the ocean, for Christ's sake?"

Charlie sat back, crossed his arms, and then stared at Peter. After a few seconds, he gave Peter the answer. "Tammy died from a bee sting."

Water sloshed from the glass that Peter was about to drink. "How did a bee get into our cabin? Explain to me how that happened." Peter looked at the two silent men. "You think I did it. You think I brought a bee onboard with me. Is that what you think?"

Charlie shrugged, "That's a good theory but no. But it did have to be someone who knew she was allergic to bees, like you, or someone you told, like Bella."

"But you just said that you didn't think that I brought a bee onboard with me."

"That's right. Someone put five …" Charlie held up his splayed right hand. "Five honey bee stingers, with their venom sacs, into her toothbrush. And to add a bit more aggravation, they rubbed peanut oil on the handle of the toothbrush and put it into the toothpaste. Your wife suffocated as her tongue swelled and her hand itched and burned like a thousand fire ants were chewing on it. Do you know anything about that, Peter, anything at all?"

Peter looked sick, his eyes were glassy, and his lips trembled as he slowly shook his head. "No. Who would want to hurt her? Who could have hated my Tammy so much that they wanted her to suffer like that? She didn't deserve to die like that." He gazed at them as tears dripped down his flushed cheeks. "You've got to find the monster who did this to my wife. Please, find this monster." His body convulsed with each gut-wrenching sob.

Charlie felt no sympathy. "I think you're the monster."

Confusion clouded Peter's face. "What? You're crazy! I didn't have anything to do with Tammy's death."

"Well, you have to see it from our side, Peter. You're the only one who knew of Tammy's allergy to bees. Either you did it or you told someone about it. Someone who wanted her dead." Charlie could see the wheels spinning in Peter's brain.

"But I didn't do it." Peter squeezed his head between his hands. "Let me think. Let me think." He began to rock as he thought. "Sophia! I think she knew." Peter snapped his finger. "Yeah, she knew. She could've done it Ask her. Go on, ask her."

Charlie flipped through his notepad. "Sophia only said that you told her of the shellfish and peanut allergy." He looked at Peter. "Nothing about bees."

"She lied."

"Why would she lie and why would she want to kill Tammy?" Charlie read his notes. "It doesn't appear that she knew your wife that well." He flipped the notepad closed. "And Sophia said she's not the least bit interested in you sexually. You're too old for her. So tell me, why she would want to kill Tammy?"

Peter chewed his well-manicured thumbnail. "My territory. That's it! She wants Puerto Rico. Sophia is framing me for the murder to get it."

"How did she get into your cabin?"

Peter threw up his hands. "What's the matter with you guys? Why are you refusing to believe that someone other than me could've been involved?"

Charlie slapped his hand on the table. "Just answer the question, Peter. How did Sophia get into your cabin?"

"I don't know, bribed the butler or that smarmy concierge with sex to let her in."

Charlie frowned, "You don't think much of your co-worker."

"Sophia is nice enough but she's a sales monkey, will do anything to get a sale. She'll do what it takes to get to Puerto Rico."

"I guess the same goes for you, too. Do whatever it takes to get Bella. But it's interesting that you should mention the concierge. Why do you think he's smarmy?"

Peter's shoulders hunched up. "He was always stopping by to talk to Tammy, asking if she needed anything, blah, blah,—"

He stopped mid-sentence, his eyebrows scrunched together. "Come to think of it, he's been our concierge for the last couple of cruises. Never gave it a second thought before now. You don't think … nah … but then again, she's the one who always booked our cruises … and he's the one who found Tammy laying on the floor. What was he doing in our cabin that late at night?"

Charlie was tired of Peter, the more the man spoke, the less he thought of him. *If Tammy was having an affair with Antonio Caruso, I can't blame her.* "Peter, you can go now. We'll be at sea tomorrow, so I don't have to tell you not to disappear."

"But what about that concierge?"

Charlie stood and walked to the door, stuck his head out, looked both ways down the hallway, and caught a glimpse of the back of Marian's head as she turned the corner toward the bank of elevators. He smiled and then turned his attention back to Peter whining about something. "I thought you said you had plans that couldn't wait? We can handle Antonio Caruso."

Peter's face brightened. "Yes, I do need to go." He glanced at his watch. "But the concierge?"

"Do you have any information about him that may be of some use? I mean, it just dawned on you that he's been your concierge for several cruises, and your wife was friends with him, apparently really good friends. Not very observant, I'd say."

Peter's cheeks flushed.

Charlie waved him out the door. "I didn't think so. But be prepared to answer more questions. Have a good night."

He opened his mouth to speak and then decided against it. Peter pushed past Charlie, almost ran into Henry, and then disappeared down the hallway.

"Good afternoon, sir." Henry bowed slightly to Charlie who walked with him to the conference table. "Good afternoon, Officer Watson."

Watson remained seated, "Hello, Henry, please take a seat unless you would like to pour yourself a glass of water."

"That is very kind of you sir." Henry sat down and waited silently for the interview to begin.

Charlie began, "Henry, you do know why we've called you here?"

"Yes, sir. To ask me questions concerning the death of Mrs. Ferguson."

"That's right. I know you are very busy; I'll try to make this quick."

Henry nodded.

Charlie opened his notepad. "When was the last time that you saw Mrs. Ferguson alive?"

"That would be at ten twenty-five. She rang me, asking for more towels and a bottle of merlot."

Charlie grinned, "That's rather precise, are you sure about the time?"

"Yes, sir, I am sure. I keep a time log so that I may anticipate requests." Henry pulled a tiny navy blue journal from his breast pocket, handing it to Charlie.

Quickly, scanning each page, Charlie noticed nothing of consequence, just columns of dates, times, cabin numbers, and requirements, such as flowers, cookies, soda, sheets, and other such innocuous requests. He found Tammy's request for towels and wine, the time noted was 9:32/10:25 PM.

"You received her call at nine thirty-two and you delivered the items to her cabin at ten twenty-five?" Charlie saw not one hint of emotion in the butler's face.

"Yes, sir, that is correct."

"And you didn't see her the rest of the night."

"No, sir."

Charlie tapped the pen on the notepad. "Did you do anything else for Mrs. Ferguson while you were there?"

"Yes, sir, I did. Mrs. Ferguson asked me to pick up a small bit of green paper, which I believe was a mint wrapper, and place it into the trashcan. She asked me to open the wine and freshen up a bowl of trail mix. The last thing I did, as per her request, was to remove the used towels and replace them with the ones I had brought."

"Did you bring the trail mix to the room? I didn't see that written down in your journal."

"No, sir. Mrs. Ferguson asked me to retrieve a plastic bag from the closet's top shelf. According to Mrs. Ferguson, she made it herself."

Charlie looked at Watson. "Do you remember seeing a plastic bag in the room?"

Henry answered instead. "No, sir, you would not have seen one. Mrs. Ferguson asked me to take it with me and dispose of it."

Charlie thought it was strange that Tammy would ask him to take the bag with him. So far, Henry added to the facts was Tammy was alive at 10:25 and he was the one to put the wrapper in the trash. "Did Mrs. Ferguson say that she was expecting anyone?"

"No, sir, but I did suspect she was."

Charlie sighed. *Why do I have to pry the information from him? Can't he just tell me everything at once?* "Henry, can you please tell me everything that you saw, heard, or did that night, all at once?" He saw a slight twitch at the corner of Henry's left cheek.

"Of course sir. I noticed a negligée laying on the bed. She had recently bathed, hence the fresh towels, and she was only wearing a robe, tightly closed of course. She also had asked me to set out two wine glasses. I asked madam if she was expecting Mr. Ferguson to return soon."

Charlie found his question to Tammy amusing. "Why did you ask her that?"

"Simple, I saw Mr. Ferguson in the lounge when I went to retrieve the bottle of merlot Mrs. Ferguson had requested. Bella was sitting with him. I found it strange that he was there, drinking with her and not with his wife." Henry looked uncomfortable. "I must admit that I was being nosy." He looked squarely at Watson, "I do apologize, Officer Watson for my insolence."

"No problem, Henry. What did Mrs. Ferguson say when you asked her?" Watson thought Henry was being a bit dramatic.

"Thank you, sir. Well, she laughed at first and said he kept vampire hours; he would be dragging his corpse to bed at daylight. Then, I assume, she realized her slip of the tongue, you know the two wine glasses because all of a sudden she stopped laughing and told me I was being rude for asking such a personal question."

Charlie chuckled, "That's a good one, vampire hours. I like that. So you left after that?"

"Yes, sir."

Charlie looked at Watson, "Got any questions for him?"

Watson shook his head. "Henry, you may go. Thank you for your time. You've been most helpful."

"Ah, I just thought of another question, Henry. Do you mind?" Charlie watched Henry hovering over his seat. "Please sit. It may take a few minutes."

He obeyed.

"Thank you. My question is, why were you following Bella and Mr. Ferguson onshore today?"

Henry looked longingly at the water sitting on the buffet.

Charlie followed his gaze, stood, walked over to the buffet, and then poured a glass of water and drank it. "Would you like a glass, Henry?" He held up his empty glass.

Henry thought twice about accepting a glass of water. With the decision made, his face became devoid of all expression, like a blank canvas. "No, thank you."

Charlie shrugged, refilled his glass and then sat in front of Henry as he drank the cold water. "Please satisfy my curiosity."

"I was only at the restaurant to speak to a friend."

Tugging his ear, Charlie clicked his tongue. "That may be, but I asked why you were following them."

Henry studied Charlie's body language, wondering if he was just shooting in the dark. "So you and your wife were following me. How else would you know?"

"You're a very smart young man, Henry." Charlie nodded.

Smiling, Henry decided to say just enough to make the detective happy. "The reason is simple. As you know, Bella and I grew up together. Our mothers were best of friends, working in the same restaurant."

"I don't see that as a reason to intrude on their privacy."

"Please, let me finish. I promised her mother that I would look out for Bella whenever I could, meaning when we are on the same ship."

Charlie shook his head, "Still not a good enough reason." He saw Henry's face tighten and wondered why he was getting upset. Was it because he didn't like being questioned or because he wasn't clever enough not to be caught spying or maybe because he wasn't a convincing liar?

"Bella is a very naïve girl, hoping to find a prince charming, she thinks every man who tosses her a smile is in love with her." Henry sighed heavily. "I am afraid her mother was the same after her husband left her; always searching for someone to whisk her away to a life of luxury."

Flipping through his pad, Charlie found the page with Bella's interview notes. "Bella said her father died. Is that what you meant when you said left?"

"No. Bella was about six-years-old when he abandoned them."

"Did her mother tell her that he had died?" Charlie was curious why Bella would lie about such a thing.

"No, she knew the truth." Henry twisted his head, making his neck pop.

Charlie thought for a few seconds. "Hmm, do you know why her father left, any explanation ever given?"

"Only rumors. I mean, only her mother and father know the real reason." Henry rubbed his cheek as if feeling for stubble. "Maybe, perhaps her grandmother knew. But the story goes is that he got tired of her demands, her other … desires. Bella's mother was never happy, even though they lived in a nice house, drove a new car, you know, things like that. She wanted more and maybe she thought some other man could give her what her husband could not. I do not know." Henry hunched his shoulders and threw up his hands. "Like I said, only rumors."

Scratching his temple with his index finger, Charlie thought about what Henry revealed. "So her mother never remarried."

"No."

"What about the other man?"

Henry shrugged. "Only rumors, there may not have been another man. Like I said, only rumors."

"What happened to Bella and her mother? Did the husband leave them penniless?"

"Not exactly. Bella's mother had enough to survive but she and Bella moved in with her own mother. I guess she wanted more and went to work, that is when she met my mother."

"And you heard these rumors from who?"

"My grandmother. I lived with my mother and grandmother."

Charlie tilted his head. "Just like Bella. What happened to your father?"

"Yes, just like Bella. My father was killed in a car accident right before I met Bella." Henry's face lit up. "Bella was like a bright star, always smiling and laughing. She helped me through a difficult time."

Looking at Henry, Charlie wondered why, according to Marian, Bella would tease him. He seemed like a nice enough guy. "Were you and Bella ever more than friends?"

Henry's face darkened. "Once, for a very short time, we decided if did not feel right. We were more like brother and sister." He tapped his watch without looking at it.

Charlie noticed the tapping. "Are we keeping you from something?"

His hand jerked away from his watch. "No, sir, just normal duties that is all."

"You'll be free to go as soon as you answer my question. Why were you following Mr. Ferguson and Bella?"

"I do not wish to speak ill of any of my guests but Mr. Ferguson is … how shall I put it politely…" Henry searched for the words and then finding them he continued, "He is not a gentleman. Bella deserves better than him. I want to protect her. That is why I was following her, to make sure Mr. Ferguson did not take advantage of her. I am sure you know what I am saying."

It dawned on Charlie that Henry never spoke with contractions. He wondered if Henry did it on purpose; if Henry thought it made him look refined. He knew Henry didn't attend college, going to work for the cruise line straight out of high school. *I wonder if he's trying to mask a lack of education or if it's just a quirk.* "Do you think if Mr. Ferguson did try to take advantage of Bella that she would mind? I mean, you said she was looking for a prince charming. Maybe he's what she wants and Bella is what he needs for him to become a gentleman. If so, who are you to interfere? Have you ever thought about that, Henry?"

Charlie saw Henry's ears pull back, nostrils flaring, and his back stiffen. He didn't want to protect Bella. He wanted Bella. Then he witnessed Henry relax.

"Perhaps, you are correct, sir, I have not thought about it that way. I see my error now. I will let Bella make her own mistakes. Thank you, sir, for enlightening me. Do you have any further questions?"

Charlie clicked his tongue. "Yep, Bella's a grown woman. If she does make any mistakes, I'm sure you'll be a good friend and help her pick up the pieces." He eased back into the chair. "I think that's all the questions I have for now." Charlie stood, walked to the door, and then surveyed up and down the hallway. *Marian's quick, nowhere in sight.*

"Thank you, sir." Henry bowed slightly to Watson and Charlie before exiting the room.

Charlie looked down the hallway. Henry was gone but Marian was sashaying toward him with a big grin on her face.

"That man is so full of it. Enlighten, my foot." Marian rolled her eyes.

Charlie kissed her on the forehead. "So you picked up on that, too?"

She walked toward the buffet. "What about you? Did you believe he saw the error of his ways?"

Watson leaned back into the chair, pushing his arms overhead, and straightening his legs. "I think it was a load of tosh." He bent forward, slapping his thighs, he stood and stretched. "And I think we should be keeping an eye on the boy."

"He definitely has a thing for Bella, not sure how healthy it is, and he definitely doesn't like Peter." Charlie refilled his glass, handing it to Marian.

Marian sipped the water and wrinkled her nose. "Needs some lemon but back to the point, just because he doesn't like Peter and he has some kind of weird obsession with Bella, doesn't seem like any reason to kill Tammy. Which by the way, I don't think he was particularly too fond of either."

Charlie ran his hand over his mouth and around to the back of his neck and squeezed it. "I have too much information right now. I need some time to sort it all out. Plus, Antonio Caruso will be here in a few minutes to add to all of this madness." He paced around the table, pausing when he reached Marian, took the glass from her hand, drank some water, and continued to pace. "And I need to question Bella and Peter again, too many conflicting statements."

"Sit down, Charlie. Let me rub your shoulders while you wait for Antonio. You look all tense, shoulders all bunched up."

Charlie quickly obeyed.

Watson grunted. "You lucky old sod."

"Quit whining, Watson. Marian doesn't mind giving your shoulders a quick squeeze." Charlie pointed a finger of warning to him. "Just don't enjoy it too much."

"Agreed."

Chapter 19

"Did you hear that?" Marian cocked her head toward the conference room door. "It sounded like someone knocked on the door."

Charlie took a few long strides and swung open the door.

A small thin man jumped back mouse-like, "Eek!"

"Are you Antonio Caruso?" Charlie stood in disbelief. He had imagined a tall, dark, and virile Italian stud, and almost laughed at what he saw. No wonder Peter Ferguson was stunned to think that his wife may have been having an affair with him.

Standing before him was a man, about five foot six, maybe seven with his shoes on, weighing about one hundred forty-five pounds, with salt and pepper hair.

Marian stepped around Charlie. "Hello, Antonio, so nice to see you again."

The frightened man dropped his hands from a rabbit-like position, his panicked expression softened with Marian's gentle greeting and her soft touch on his forearm. "Good afternoon, madam, always a pleasure to see you." He bowed, taking her hand in both of his, holding it for a few seconds.

"Thank you, Antonio, you are so kind."

He relinquished her hand with a slight nod.

"I must be off. Just stopped by to see my darling husband." Marian turned, giving Charlie a wink and a peck on the cheek. She waved to Antonio as she breezed past.

Charlie had no recollection of the man who stood before him. But it was apparent that Marian knew him well. He was going to ask Marian about that or better yet, ask Antonio. *Maybe he's one of these guys that conveniently waits for the husband to leave and then swoops in with his little boy charm.* He didn't worry about Marian falling for that act.

He extended his hand toward the meek man. "I'm glad to meet you, Antonio Caruso." Charlie released Antonio's surprisingly firm grip. "Please come, help yourself to some water, if you'd like, and take a seat."

The concierge poured two glasses of water, drank half of one, refilled it and then sat down, crossing his arms and legs.

Two glasses of water? He must think he'll be here for a while. Yep, he definitely looks like a possum caught in the middle of the road, frightened, and confused, not knowing what to do. Charlie could have felt sorry for the poor guy, if not for the grisly murder. "Mr. Caruso, I understand you found Mrs. Ferguson's body."

Antonio wiped sweat from his upper lip. "Yes."

Charlie licked his dry lips and sighed thinking, *this is going to be painfully long if he continues with single word answers.* "Will you please elaborate with maybe the time, why you were there, what you did when you found her?"

"Yes." Antonio drained one of the glasses and grimaced as if he had just downed a glass of cheap whiskey. "It was about twelve-thirty, maybe a little later, but definitely after midnight for sure."

"For sure, why?"

Antonio shifted in his chair, looking very uncomfortable. "Officer Watson, please understand, I love my job. If I tell you the whole truth, will you promise me that you will not have me dismissed?"

Officer Watson looked at Charlie.

"It's your ship, your rules, Watson."

He considered Antonio's request. "I can only give you that promise if you tell us the truth and you haven't broken any laws. Now, you may be written up for misconduct on the ship. I can't promise that won't happen."

Antonio believed his superior. "Thank you, sir. I will not lose my job. No laws have I broken, none."

"Well, then, tell us about that night. Spare no details." Watson retrieved the untouched water pitcher, refilling Antonio's glass. He sat the pitcher on the table, figuring at this rate, Antonio was going to empty it.

Charlie watched Antonio struggle to collect his thoughts, hopefully, truthful ones.

The concierge put his hand over his mouth, took several deep breaths through his nose, and then began his story. "I have known Ta … Mrs. Ferguson for many years now. We met during one of her many cruises."

"Did she always book cruises knowing you would be her concierge?" Charlie scribbled down Antonio's statement.

"Yes, we kept in touch after the first time we met. I would give her my schedule with each new contract I signed."

"How long do your contracts usually last?"

"Six months."

Charlie knew the answer to his next question but he had to hear it from Antonio. "Were you and Tammy Ferguson lovers?"

Antonio held up his head, not ashamed of his answer. "Yes, but we were very discreet. No one suspected anything."

"How do you know that? How can you be absolutely sure no one knew about your relationship?"

He chuckled. "You've never worked on a cruise ship or you'd know that the crew lives for gossip. There's not much more to do. If anyone so much as thought, suspected, dreamed that I was sleeping with her, the whole ship would have been on fire about it. Believe me, I would have known." Antonio reached for his glass, "As far as her husband was concerned, he was clueless, too caught up in his own affairs, never gave her a second thought."

Looking at Antonio, Charlie tried to figure out what it was about the concierge that had drawn Tammy to him. *Maybe his Italian accent? He does have a nice smile, straight, white teeth, and a good thick head of hair. I guess a woman might say he's cute, in a lost puppy dog way, with his big brown eyes. Or maybe it was because he simply cared for her.*

"When did your affair start?" Charlie wondered how long Peter had been in the dark concerning his wife's other life.

"We met thirty years ago but the affair didn't start until about twenty years ago."

Officer Watson coughed.

Antonio hung his head and clasped his hands together on top of the table, his fingers turned white.

Charlie wondered if he was squeezing his hands together so hard in an effort to keep himself from falling apart. "Twenty years is a long time. Did you ever talk about getting married?"

Antonio smirked. "At first, but I have nothing to offer her, I stay on with this cruise line to see her. Besides she's … was happy with the way things were." He sniffed and brought his hands to his lap, fidgeting with his fingers.

Charlie remembered when he first met Marian how difficult it was not to think about her, wanting to be with her all the time. Not being with her for months at a time would be pure hell. "Did you love her?"

Leaning forward, Antonio grabbed the pitcher of water, refilled his glass and held it, not drinking. He blinked his eyes several times, fighting his tears. "Yes, I did and I know what you're thinking, that she was just using me."

Not wanting to rub salt into Antonio's fresh wounds, Charlie sat in silence. He could tell that Antonio wanted to talk, so he waited patiently for the heartbroken man to continue.

"I didn't care. Tammy was beautiful in so many ways, so full of vitality, nurturing, tender, and loving. I loved everything about her."

"So, you're sure she didn't love you." Charlie was mystified why Tammy didn't want to be with Antonio forever. The man truly loved her.

"She said that she had made a vow. She said the way things were between us, made our time together sweeter, more precious, and exciting. It gave her something to dream about, something to get her through the daily drudge with Peter."

"But you didn't believe her?"

"I don't know." Antonio stared at the floor. "I think she truly cared for me, probably loved me, too, in her own way, but the money ..." He looked at Charlie. "I feel like that was keeping us apart. She had grown accustomed to that way of life."

Charlie sighed heavily. *Greed, look what it got her.* "Tell me about that day, step by step."

"The morning was uneventful. She called me after Bella made up the room and Peter announced he wanted to go into town to bar hop."

"I take it Tammy had no interest in that."

Antonio smiled, "No, she was a true lady. She went to the ship's spa instead. Tammy wanted to lunch together in the suite but I told her it was too risky. So we planned to spend a few hours together after they dined and Peter left for the bar."

"Did Tammy tell Bella where Peter would be that night?"

He nodded. "In an around about way. When they passed Bella on their way to dinner, Tammy made sure Bella overheard her tell Peter to feel free to go to the bar without her after dinner."

Charlie scratched the back of his head. "She knew Bella was interested in Peter. Was Peter interested in Bella, too?"

"Any idiot could see that Bella was hot for Peter and he was happy with any female that fell for his charm. He was easy prey for Bella."

"Prey? She does this often, I mean, seduces men?"

"Every now and then." Antonio paused, "Come to think of it, just rich, older Americans." He squeezed his chin with his right hand and chuckled. "As a matter of fact, they all kind of look like Peter."

Charlie glanced at Officer Watson and wondered if he was thinking the same thing. Was there a connection with Peter and Bella's mother? Maybe Bella even had a little blackmail scheme going on since it seemed to be a habit of hers, seducing rich, older men. He made a note in his notepad.

"Once Tammy made sure Bella knew of Peter's after dinner plans, then what happened?"

"They went to dinner, returned to the suite. Our plan was for me to come to the suite at eleven-thirty."

Charlie interrupted Antonio, "Why eleven-thirty?"

"She wanted to get ready for me; you know what women do, shower, shave, things like that. Then after she showered, she would have the soiled linens taken away just in case Peter gave a second thought to why she showered again. Tammy would also order a bottle of merlot, our favorite. Eleven-thirty would give us plenty of time for Peter and Henry to be gone. Plus, all of the cabins would have been turned down, so no maids or stewards would be hanging around in the hallway and most of the guests would be in their cabins or somewhere drinking."

Charlie nodded. He knew the timing was off because according to Doctor Nelson, Antonio banged on his door around one o'clock in the morning. Jack estimated that Tammy died around eleven o'clock. "I guess you've been doing this long enough to know when you'd have the all clear. Did you arrive on time?"

"No, at the last minute, I was asked to tend bar, which was around ten o'clock. Bella was supposed to relieve me at midnight. I called Tammy a few minutes after eleven but she didn't answer. I just assumed she had ..." Antonio's voice trailed into silence, he turned his head and stared at the water in the bottom of the pitcher sitting on the buffet.

Officer Watson gave Antonio a napkin from the buffet.

Charlie provided Antonio a minute to regain his composure. "You said Bella was supposed to relieve you at midnight. What happened?"

Antonio pressed the napkin to his eyes, and then wiped his nose. "When she didn't show up at midnight, I asked one of the waitresses who was about to go off duty if she'd find Bella for me. The waitress said that was easy enough, and then told me Bella was in the corner with some old man. I knew the old man had to be Peter." Antonio's voice began louder.

"Around what time was that?" Charlie now knew Bella had lied and so had Peter.

"Twelve-fifteen, maybe later." Antonio twisted the napkin into the shape of a small snake.

Charlie jotted down the time. "You couldn't see the table from the bar?"

"No, it's in a dark, back corner. I went over there and sure enough, there was Bella glued to Peter. Peter was so drunk, he didn't even know who I was. Not that I even cared. Bella glared at me and stormed over to the bar." Antonio tossed the deformed napkin onto the table.

Charlie remembered Henry saying that he saw Bella as he passed through the bar to get the merlot. But if she was in an out-of-the-way corner, he couldn't have seen her in passing. "So Bella was supposed to tend bar at midnight and was not waiting tables before then."

"Yes, to bartending, and no, she was not waiting tables, at least not in my bar or I would've seen her."

"But you don't know how long she was in the corner with Peter."

"No. All I know is that she was not behind the bar at midnight."

Charlie drummed his fingers on the table. "Hmm, interesting. Did you see Henry in the bar?"

"Yes, he came into the bar to get a bottle of merlot for Tammy. That was around ten-fifteen or so." Antonio grunted, "Our bottle." He picked up the twisted napkin, opened it, and blotted his eyes, again.

"Did Henry say anything or do anything unusual?"

Antonio shook his head, "He asked for the bottle. I got it, filled out a ticket, he left."

Charlie cleared his throat. "Okay, let me see if I have this straight. You had to tend bar unexpectedly and Bella was to take over at midnight but she was late because she was with Peter. And Henry came in around ten-fifteen to get the wine. The last time you spoke with Tammy was before lunch?"

"No, I spoke to her after Peter arrived from his shore excursion and he was in the shower. That's when we firmed up our plans."

Charlie dreaded the next part of the interview, finding Tammy's body. "Antonio, we need to know what happened after you left the bar."

Antonio took a deep breath, held it for a couple of seconds before exhaling. "Normally, I would serpentine through the ship, stopping by my cabin before going to her suite. But because I was running late, I only took a few turns before heading to her suite."

"Did you pass anyone in the hallway leading to her suite?"

"No."

Charlie had hoped Antonio may have unknowingly seen the killer. "How did you get into the suite?"

Antonio smiled weakly, "I'm their concierge; I have a key. So do Henry and Bella." He looked at Officer Watson, "Isn't that right? Did I miss anyone?"

Officer Watson agreed. "No, those are the only members of the staff that have access to that suite. Well, security has access but only if there's an emergency."

Charlie groaned inside. He felt that they were no closer to solving this crime. "Okay, once inside, what did you see? Take your time." He watched Antonio's expression as he re-lived that moment.

"I opened the door as quietly as I could. All the lights were on, the water was running in the bathroom sink. I remember thinking how strange that was because it was the only sound I heard. Then I saw her lying on the floor." Antonio reached for one of the water glasses, held it with both hands, and drank it dry.

"Take your time. Would you like some more water?"

Officer Watson didn't wait for an answer, refilling all of their glasses.

Antonio held the glass but didn't drink. "I ran to her side." His face screwed up. "Her face … was swollen. I wasn't sure it was her. She wasn't moving, I grabbed her hand and patted it. Then I shook her shoulders, begged her to wake up, to speak to me. She wasn't responding, not moving, so I leaned over, put my head on her chest to listen for a heartbeat. I panicked, there wasn't one. I just ran out of the room to get Doctor Nelson."

"Who told Peter?"

"I did. She's still his wife. He had to know."

Charlie wondered how difficult it must have been for him to tell Peter that his wife was dead. Antonio's heart had been crushed by Tammy's death, yet it would be Peter who would be consoled. No wonder Antonio disappeared after telling Peter. He needed the solitude to pour out his own hidden grief.

"How did Peter react when you told him about Tammy?"

Antonio shook his head and smirked. "I told him that his wife was ill but he was so drunk, he didn't understand what I said and he laughed."

"Laughed? What on earth did he think you said?" Charlie felt his anger warm the back of his neck.

Antonio gritted his teeth. "I wanted to punch him in the face." He slammed his fist into the palm of his hand. "I wanted to tell him Tammy deserved better than him. That I was the man she loved, not him." His voice died as he stared with watery eyes at Charlie. "I want my Tammy back," Antonio whispered.

Charlie swallowed the lump that had formed in his throat. *I've only loved Marian for just over three months and I think I would die if something ... I can't even think it. How will I cope after twenty years?*

"Who did this to my Tammy?" Antonio moaned, "Why would anybody want to kill her? Why?" He wiped away the tears from his cheeks. "Why make her suffer? Who hated her so much?" Antonio's chin rested on his chest, his hands hiding his eyes, but nothing could hide his pain.

Officer Watson and Charlie waited in silence for Antonio's hurt to subside.

"I'm sorry but I loved her. Please ... please find who did this to her. Please."

Charlie stared into Antonio's eyes. "We'll do all we can but we still need some help from you."

Antonio dipped his head. "Whatever you need."

"What did you say to Peter to make him understand the gravity of the situation?"

"I looked right at him and said, your wife is dead." Antonio snorted, "Peter thought I was joking. He looked at me and said, get out of my face. I said, what's the matter with you? Your wife is dead! Don't you even care?"

"What did he say?"

"I could see his mind processing my words. Once reality sank in, he jumped up and ran toward his suite. And me, I went to my cabin and prayed I was having a nightmare."

Charlie looked away from Antonio's private anguish and wished he could give the broken man some peace by finding Tammy's killer. "Antonio, did you know of Tammy's allergy to bees?"

He shook his head. "No. I only know ... knew of her allergy to peanuts and seafood."

Scribbling in his pad, Charlie wondered if anyone other than Peter Ferguson knew of Tammy's bee allergy. But then again, who could he believe?

Chapter 20

"Mmm, I love junk food." Marian popped into her mouth the last bite of a fried mozzarella stick. She sighed, "But I guess it loves me too; it clings to my thighs."

She gazed at the stars, the sea breezes toyed with her hair. Marian was truly happy. Happy she was Mrs. Charlie McClung, never dreaming she'd ever be anything other than Marian Selby, Lee's widow. She wondered if Peter was experiencing any tugs of anguish because the woman who shared 35 years of his life was gone. She closed her eyes, thankful for the man that was now in her life.

Marian looked at Charlie. He was staring at her, a lopsided smile on his lips. "What?"

"I love watching the many moods of you."

A quizzical look took control of Marian's expression. "What do you mean, the many moods of me?"

"You know happy, sad, contended. When you were looking up at the stars, I saw your expression change rapidly, in just a few seconds. A smile was on your face, and then it faltered as if you were sad. You closed your eyes and sighed, then the happy smile returned." He reached for the clump of hair that had strayed from behind her ear, tucking it safely away. "I'm one lucky man."

Marian sighed heavily, "How does love go so wrong?"

"You're thinking about the Fergusons and Antonio?"

"Yeah, and I know I'm not supposed to be dwelling on things like that in our honeymoon suite." Marian squeezed her husband's hand, "But I can't help it. I feel our love and I can't imagine it ever tumbling over an abyss like theirs did."

Charlie rolled out of his padded chaise lounge and onto Marian's, snuggling close to his wife, and feeling as if they were one body. "They let it happen. People have choices and they chose unwisely." He pressed his nose into Marian soft hair and inhaled its clean scent. "The only one I feel sorry for is Antonio."

"Poor, Antonio. He truly loved Tammy and Tammy …" Marian fought back tears and pulled Charlie's arms tighter around her slender body. "I was like Tammy when I first met you. I was afraid to let go of something that was gone, afraid to venture into the unknown."

"Ah, but you chose wisely." Charlie felt Marian tremble as she giggled and then he kissed the back of her neck.

"Mmm, I like it when you kiss me there."

Charlie released her and stood over her. "What would you say, if I picked you up and tossed you onto the bed?"

"I'd say have your way with me, big boy." Marian stretched her arms toward him.

He picked her up and was about to step through the open sliding glass doors when he heard voices coming from the Ferguson's suite.

"Did you hear that?"

Marian whispered, "Yes. Sounds like an argument."

Charlie let Marian down slowly. "Yeah." He crept inside, pressed his ear on the wall that they and the Fergusons shared, and motioned Marian to join him.

"Sounds like Peter and … Bella?"

Charlie nodded, "Yeah, Watson must have released the suite back to Peter."

"Why?"

"No reason not to, we searched it thoroughly. Peter probably needs underwear."

Marian rolled her eyes and stifled a laugh. "Bella sounds pretty pissed about something."

"Wait, sounds like someone opened the sliding glass doors." Charlie snuck out onto their balcony. Marian shadowed him.

"Will you calm down, Bella? Nobody thinks that you killed Tammy, besides you have an alibi, me and a hundred other people in the bar."

Charlie could hear ice cubes clinking in a glass.

"Then tell me why they want to talk to me, again? Huh, tell me!"

Bella must have shoved Peter because he heard Peter swear and the sound of furniture sliding across the balcony.

"You stupid heifer, do you how much this scotch cost? Damn it, you better hope it doesn't ruin this silk shirt!"

"Or what? My life isn't worth as much as your wife's?"

Charlie heard Peter slam down the glass on the table.

"Shut up! Someone might hear you."

Bella let out a small scream and then Charlie heard the thud of a body hitting the floor.

"That's it. I'm going over there."

Before Marian could move to follow him, she heard loud banging on the Ferguson's cabin door.

"This is Detective McClung. Open this door right now!"

The door swung open as Marian stumbled into Charlie.

Peter stood with his hand high on the door, the other hand holding a glass with ice cubes and a finger of golden liquid. The majority of the liquid appeared to be a jellyfish-shaped stain on his Hawaiian shirt. A sneer was plastered on his face. "Jeez, will you ever let me enjoy my cruise?"

Marian practically lunged at Peter. Charlie held her back as she lashed out at the drunken man. "Enjoy your cruise! Your wife is dead and all you can think about is your own pleasure? Really? You're nothing but a ..."

Charlie interrupted his wife. "I heard a woman scream and what sounded like someone falling on the floor." Charlie looked around Peter and saw Bella pretending to clean the room. "Are you all right, Bella?"

"Yes, sir. Clumsy me, I tripped over a chair leg." Bella avoided looking directly at Charlie.

Charlie smirked, "Bella, where's your cleaning cart? Did someone move it?" He saw Bella stiffen.

"I just got back my suite." Peter jerked his thumb over his shoulder. "Saw the girl there in the hallway and asked her to tidy up this dusty cabin." Peter drained his glass. "She only came in to see which cleaning supplies she needed before lugging that contraption down the hallway."

Bella breezed past them. "I'll return in a few moments to turn down the bed and freshen up the bathroom."

Peter turned away from the door and walked toward a bottle of scotch sitting on the coffee table. "Can I offer you one?" He held up the dark bottle.

Charlie stepped inside the suite, looked around for any changes or anything of interest that he may have missed from the search. The bathroom was still in disarray, the wilted flowers sat on the dresser, the open bottle of merlot now sat beside the flowers clinging for life on the end table. Tammy's negligée was gone but her shoes remained beside the bed. And the trail mix was nowhere in sight.

"I like a glass of scotch every now and then if it's decent." Charlie took the bottle Peter offered him and read the label. "Aberfeldy 21, not bad. It's been a while since I've had a glass of this." He gave the bottle to Peter. "I like my scotch neat."

"Damn right, this stuff is the best." Peter splashed about three fingers into an old fashioned tumbler.

Charlie inhaled the single malt, a weak honey scent, ripe fruit, and malty overtone. The taste was smooth and sweet, flavors of heather and honey with a hint of vanilla were taken over by lemon and orange, and then honey and ripe fruit returned, lingering on his tongue. "Ah, it finishes nicely."

Marian stood halfway hidden behind Charlie. "May I have a sip?"

"I'll pour you a glass." Peter reached for another tumbler.

"No, I just want a taste. I'm not the great connoisseur like my husband." She sipped from Charlie's glass, swallowed, and then pursed her lips. Marian sucked air in through her open mouth, exhaled quickly. "I must say, it's smoother than the stuff Da had, but it still tastes like kerosene."

The two men laughed.

Peter offered them a seat. Marian sat down. Charlie was slow to sit, took another sip of scotch and waited for Peter to sit first before settling beside his wife.

Peter leaned forward, rested his elbows on his thighs, held his glass with both hands as he stared at the dying flowers on the dresser. "I've been an ass." He sat up, started to set down the drink but instead, collapsed back on the loveseat with a heavy sigh and stared at Charlie and Marian.

"I have to agree with you," Charlie replied.

Marian returned Peter's gaze. "Why? Have you always been an ass or is this how you're coping with Tammy's death?"

Peter snorted. "I like you." He saluted Marian with his glass, then drank. "I guess I've always been one to a certain degree but now … now …" His eyes shifted toward the ceiling. "Now, I think you're right. It's my way of coping. I grieved the night she died, cried like a girl. But I'm done. Nothing can bring her back. Right now, I just want to forget."

"What, like she never existed?"

Charlie was impressed with his wife's interviewing skills. *She probably doesn't realize what she's doing. A natural she is. A natural.*

"Boy, you go right for the jugular." Peter topped off his drink. "I can't ever forget Tammy. She was a huge part of my life but I'm not going to dwell on the fact that she's gone. I mean what good would it do?"

Marian gasped and clutched Charlie's thigh, unconsciously dug in her nails. "Don't you even feel just a little bit sad that she's gone?"

Peter grabbed the bottle of Aberfeldy, shook it in the air. "Numbs the senses. Gotta love the stuff." He offered to pour more into Charlie's tumbler.

He waved him away. "No, I've got plenty."

Peter shrugged.

Marian was silent.

Charlie slowly rubbed Marian's upper back; she released her death grip from his thigh. "So, tell me the real reason Bella was here." He held the glass to his lips but didn't drink, never taking his eyes from Peter.

"Frankly, I'm not sure. She must have been following me because no sooner had I shut the door, she was knocking on it."

"I overheard you two arguing and I heard Bella fall on the floor. Did you push her? Tell me the truth, because I'm going to ask her."

Peter hunched up his shoulders. "Not exactly, she backed away from me and tripped over the door track."

"What did you do to make her so afraid that she needed to get away from you?"

He smirked and pointed to his wet shirt. "This is a twenty dollar stain, not counting the cost of the shirt and having it cleaned. I got angry and may have given her the idea I was going to hit her."

Marian clicked her tongue. "You'd hurt someone over spilled scotch?"

Peter cleared his throat and rubbed his eye. "Uh, Tammy gave me this shirt and the scotch. Bella had no right to ruin it."

"So you do have a heart." Marian smiled and felt relieved that Peter had redeemed himself somewhat, in a roundabout way, admitting that he still cared for Tammy, that he had not so quickly banished her from his memories.

Charlie heard Marian sniff and handed her a tissue.

Marian gave up trying to figure out where they came from but was glad he always had a tissue when she needed one. She dabbed the corner of her eyes and blotted her nose.

"Why was Bella so angry with you?"

Peter considered his options, tell the truth or feign ignorance again. "You probably heard what she said. She accused me of telling lies about her because you guys want to talk to her again."

"Did you?"

He hunched up his shoulders, bobbed his head side to side, "No, not really. I mean, I found out today that I knew her mother briefly. I met her in a bar years ago after I first got the Puerto Rican territory."

Charlie thought, *now that puts a new wrinkle in the plot, definitely adds more meat to the stew.* "So how did you figure out that you knew her mother?"

"I happened to mention that she reminded me of someone but I couldn't remember who." Peter tilted back the tumbler and took a long sip. "She got all quiet and her eyes grew the size of saucers. Then she told me not to go anywhere, she had something she wanted me to look at."

"Just a minute, where were you when this happened?"

"In the cabin down below, the temporary one. Does it make a difference?"

"No, just curious. Continue."

"Bella runs from the cabin and comes back with this old black and white photo of her mother. It looked like someone had wadded up the photo, all creased and torn a bit. You know what I mean."

Charlie nodded.

"She hands it to me and says, is this you? I looked at it for a while, kind of hard to see the faces with all the cracks. But I said, yeah, it resembles me in my younger days, more hair and less belly." Peter took another sip. "I say to her, this is your mother?" He pulled his head back with a startled expression.

"What happened?"

Peter set his drink on the table. Bella turns red and starts huffing and puffing, screams, how could you forget my mother? She never stopped thinking about you." Peter threw up his hands in a defensive gesture. "I was ready for her to start smacking on me but instead, she calms down and takes a deep breath. She smiles and said, you're probably not the one. You're not exactly the knight in shining armor she talked about. She apologized then walks out."

"Was it you in the picture?"

"Yeah, but I wasn't going to admit it. Sheesh, I was afraid she'd claim I was her father, which by the way is impossible. I fooled around but never went that far with anybody in Puerto Rico. Never!"

Charlie found that somewhat hard to believe. "Why is that?"

"Too close to work. I didn't need any clinging vines around my neck."

"I'm curious," Marian suddenly spoke. "Was she married when you met her? Was Bella even born when you met?

Peter grinned, "Nah, she wasn't married and one of her friends told me that she had a kid. An unmarried woman with a kid usually makes them much more inclined to latch on to you. I don't know where this knight in shining armor crap came from." He picked up his glass and swirled it around. "I never gave anybody, ever, any reason to think that they were anything more than a one-night stand." Peter tossed back the remaining scotch in the tumbler.

This guy is a jerk, a number one jerk. I can't believe Tammy would rather stay with him instead of being with Antonio. Charlie felt like telling him so but it wouldn't be conducive to the investigation. He heard Marian mumble under her breath.

Charlie wanted to get Marian away from this guy. This was not at all what he had envisioned for this night. He got straight to the point. "Bella seems to think that you killed Tammy for her life insurance or inheritance. Which is it?"

Peter grunted, "So you heard that, too?"

"Yes, care to explain?"

"Well, I might as well come clean. You'll find out sooner or later but yeah, Tammy is … was loaded and has a hefty life insurance policy. But I didn't kill her and I don't need her money. I've got plenty and I have a hefty life insurance policy as well. You can check that out while you're at it. Besides, she had more reasons to kill me than I her. I'm a louse and I'm worth way more dead than alive."

Charlie leaned forward and set down his empty glass. "I will, but I don't understand why Bella thinks you killed your wife."

Peter offered to refill his glass. Charlie waved him away. "That, you'll have to ask her yourself. I don't have a clue but I can assure you that I did not kill my wife."

"That brings me to another question. Why did you start drinking, again?"

"Ah, I see you've been talking to Kaye. She's a nice lady, a bit pushy, but she's all right." He put the tumbler to his lips and sipped. "Just so you know, I never stopped, only slowed down." Peter grinned. "Tammy wanted me to attend the AA meetings, said my drinking was getting out of hand." He tipped the glass in Charlie's direction. "She was right. These past two months, I've saved a boat load of money just by savoring my drinks."

This is what he calls savoring. Having enough of Peter's nonsense, Charlie stood, bringing Marian up with him. "It's been a long day. Thank you for the scotch and the interesting chat. Have a good night."

Peter started to rise.

"No need to see us out. Sit and enjoy the Aberfeldy."

Peter saluted him with the bottle and refilled his glass.

"One last question, did Tammy brush her teeth before you went to dinner that night?"

Peter quickly replied, "Yes."

"Before you left to go to the bar?"

"No, but she always brushed her teeth before going to bed. Why?"

"Just curious. Have a good night."

As Charlie shut the door, he glanced back at Peter; his head was in his hands and his body jerked as the sounds of muffled crying floated in the air.

Chapter 21

"Sophia, why are you acting like this?" Jack Jackson stared at his sister as she slid her narrow feet into a pair of bright red stilettos, buckling the straps around her ankles.

She smoothed down all sides of the tight, red gown, the long slit set off-center in the front of the dress, exposing too much thigh in Jack's opinion.

"Acting like what?" Sophia leaned toward the dresser mirror as she applied deep red lipstick. She turned to look at her brother sitting on one of the two twin beds.

Jack waved his hands frantically in the air outlining his Sophia's shape. "You're acting like a two-bit floozy."

Sophia laughed, "A floozy! You sound like granddad. Floozy, really." She shook her head. "I know you're my older brother and want to protect me, but I'm a grown woman, newly divorced, who wants to have a little bit of fun before I turn into an old drudge."

Jack started to protest but decided against it, knowing his sister was more hard-headed than himself. "Fine. Are you going out with Peter again? You know he tried to throw you under the bus for Tammy's murder."

Sophia grunted, "Really, hmm." She bit her bottom lip as she fastened garnet and diamond dangle earrings to her small lobes.

"That's all you've got to say about a man who's implicated you in a murder?" Jack was stunned by his sister's passiveness.

"Calm down, really, you're a bit high strung tonight. I thought the whole point of this cruise was to help you relax."

Jack crossed his arms over his narrow chest. "Just answer the question. It doesn't bother you that your boss is trying to put the spotlight on you for his wife's death?"

"Nope." She studied the tips of her fingernails, their color matched her lips.

Jack rolled his eyes. "Now I know you're insane. I thought you were when you left your husband but now, there's no doubt."

"I know I don't have anything to do with Tammy's death and Peter knows that. He's the best sales rep in the company and how do you think he made it to the top? Hmm? By making you believe whatever he wants you to believe." She put her hands on the curve of her waist. "Man, if I could ever be that good, I could have my choice of territories."

"I don't even know you anymore, Sophia." Jack felt a deep disappointment, a sadness, that his baby sister was lost. Those he loved and thought he knew, his wife and now Sophia, were nothing but strangers to him now.

"What's the matter, Jack?" Sophia sat next to her brother, putting her arm across his back. "I'm still me but I've decided to be happy and nobody is going to take that away from me. Not anymore. What Peter said doesn't affect me because they're just words. I know they're not true and I know why Peter said them. He's a narcissistic, shallow, greedy, callous, sad excuse of a human being. Peter Ferguson is a user, a taker."

"So why do you hang around with him?"

"First of all, he's my boss and I want to climb to the top of the corporate ladder. And second, when it comes to women, he seems to be blind to the fact that they use him just as much as he uses them, if not more. He seems to think he always has the upper hand. I'm the user in the relationship with Peter."

Jack patted Sophia's knee. "Just as long as you don't become like him, don't lose your true nature, the sweet, little tomboy I grew up with."

"Promise."

Jack squeezed her knee hard.

Sophia jumped up and slapped him on the back of his head.

Jack in turn, planted his foot on her butt and gave her a little shove. "I'm still your big brother."

She dusted off her butt cheek, turning toward the mirror. "You better be glad your nasty shoe didn't leave a mark on my dress." Sophia saw Jack's reflection in the mirror. He looked troubled. Whipping around to face her brother, she asked, "What's wrong?"

"I'm worried about you. I mean, Peter may have killed his wife. She died a horrible death. Do you realize that? And if he thinks you're a threat, then what do you think he'll do?"

Sophia's mind worked on what Jack had said. "No, you don't really think that …" Her words faded as she plopped down beside Jack. "He loved Tammy in his own weird way. Why would he kill her?"

"Look, you've only known him three years. She knew him for over thirty-five years and Tammy apparently didn't think he'd kill her either."

"But you don't know it was Peter. It could have been anybody with access to their cabin, anybody." Sophia didn't want to believe her mentor could be a murderer.

Jack nodded. "Yeah, you're right but it had to be somebody who knew about Tammy's allergy to bees. Did you know about it?"

"No."

"So, why would the staff know?"

Sophia drummed her nails on her thighs as she thought. "Peter or Tammy could have said something about it in passing, you know, without thinking."

"It had to be planned. Someone brought the honey bee stingers onboard. How many bees have you seen flying around?"

Sophia's slumped. "What should I do? I can't avoid him like he's a leper."

"Are you meeting him tonight?"

She perked up. "No, I'm meeting that dishy first officer, Jameson Cornelia." Sophia rubbed her palms together.

"I thought they weren't supposed to fraternize with the guests."

"We're having a cozy little dinner, just the two of us."

"And you're dressed like that!"

Sophia playfully swatted his shoulder, "Shouldn't you be happy that I'm not meeting Peter? Whom, by the way, I will avoid to the best of my ability."

Jack pointed his finger in her face. "You just be careful, okay? I don't want to be …" He paused and swallowed his emotions. "You just be careful." Jack stood. "Well, I think I'll play undercover cop and tail Peter. Should be pretty easy, just find the happening bar, right?"

"Yeah, pretty much." Sophia looked at her delicate wristwatch. "I should be heading out. Are you okay?"

Jack handed his sister a small clutch the same color as her dress. "I'm fine. Remember … where did you get this?" Jack touched the pointed brass knuckle-like closure on the small bag.

"Yes, a handy little item, demure and deadly." She slid her fingers through the holes. "I can pack quite a wallop with this." Sophia took a boxer's stance. "You know you don't have to worry about me."

Jack began to judo chop the air. "I know we both have our jujutsu black belts but that was a long time ago. I just don't want you to get caught off guard."

"The same goes for you." She jabbed her fingernail into her brother's chest. "If Peter is a murderer and he thinks you're on to him, then he may find you a threat. Thank goodness, you're not allergic to anything."

Jack rubbed his chest. "Ouch, your talons are sharp, you old harpy."

Sophia laughed, blew on her nails and then polished them on her dress.

Chapter 22

"Ah, this reminds me of my youth back in England." Officer Watson scooped sausage, bacon, over-easy eggs, and fried potatoes on his plate. "All we're missing for a proper fry-up are the kidneys and a black and white pudding." He moved on to the next section of the buffet and loaded his plate with sliced tomatoes, fried mushrooms, beans, and a few kippers. Picking up two slices of toast, he put one on his plate and began to eat the other as he made his way to the table, choosing a seat across from Marian.

Marian wrinkled her nose at the sight of the kippers and wondered how anyone could eat beans and fish for breakfast. Her plate was a colorful palate of mixed fresh fruit, a big dollop of peach yogurt sprinkled with granola, and two slices of crispy bacon.

Charlie sat next to Marian. "You don't have enough on your plate to make a bird skinny." His plate was similar to Officer Watson's, minus the kippers and beans.

"I ate way too much last night, this is plenty. You don't want me to be getting all chubby on you do you?"

"We'll get chubby together. You'll be my chunky monkey and I'll be your chubby hubby, how about that?" Charlie popped half a sausage link into his mouth, then planted a greasy kiss on Marian's cheek.

She picked up a slice of bacon and pointed it at him, "Does this mean you'll go clothes shopping with me when I've outgrown my old ones?"

"On second thought, you have plenty on your plate and you don't need this." Charlie gently pulled the bacon out of her hand.

Jack walked by and snatched the bacon from Charlie's hand. "Always room for one more piece of bacon." He circled the table and sat next to Watson.

Doctor Nelson sat at the head of the table. "Shall we discuss the investigation as we eat or wait until we finish?" He looked at Marian for an answer.

"Now will be fine." She stood to get a cup of coffee. "Does anyone want anything while I'm up? Coffee?"

They all replied yes to the coffee.

"If you don't mind too terribly much, would you bring the toast caddy to the table?" Watson wiped crumbs from his fingertips.

Marian set down the caddy, along with a small basket of assorted jams and a chilled saucer of butter curls. "I thought you might want these, too."

"Mrs. Mc … I mean, Marian, you are most thoughtful. McClung, I can see why you married her."

Charlie pointed his fork at Officer Watson. "Every morning when I wake up and see her lying beside me, I send up a prayer of thanks that she hasn't come to her senses and left me."

"Oh, Charlie, why would I leave the most practically perfect man on Earth?" Marian set down the pot of coffee and hugged him from behind, kissing the top of his head.

All the men made gagging noises.

"So it's true, love is blind." Officer Watson said nonchalantly as he buttered a slice of toast.

Marian laughed, "You guys are terrible. I think love reveals and it revealed this absolutely marvelous man to me." She kissed him again.

"Thank you, sweetie." With a smug grin, Charlie raised his cup of coffee. "Here's to true love. It's definitely worth the wait."

Doctor Nelson raised his cup with Charlie. "Here's to love and all that stuff, blah, blah, blah. Now gentlemen, madam, let's get on with business."

Marian blushed slightly and continued to refill everyone's cup.

"We've got one more interesting tidbit," Doctor Nelson paused as Marian topped off his coffee. He lightly touched her hand and smiled. "Thank you and I apologize for my rudeness."

"I understand." She returned the nearly empty pot to the buffet, and then returned to sit next to Charlie.

"Jack, do you want to explain your findings?"

"Sure," Jack was leaning against the buffet, within arm's reach of the bacon. "We know someone put peanut oil on the toothbrush and in the paste. Now, this is the weird thing, they laced the peanut oil with DMSO making it even more potent. That explains the severity of the rash on her hands, and it probably exacerbated the swelling." He selected a long piece of bacon and began to chew on it.

"So are you now saying she died from the peanut oil?" Charlie pushed away his empty plate, rested his forearms on the table, and then leaned forward.

"No," Jack mumbled around a mouth full of bacon. He washed it down with a glass of orange juice. "She definitely died because of the stingers."

"Wait a minute," Marian interrupted. "What is DMSO?"

"A simple explanation is it's a type of liniment that can penetrate the skin without damaging it and anything you mix with it enters your body too. The only reason I looked for DMSO was that slight hint of garlic on her hand, which is characteristic of DMSO." Jack grinned. "You can kill someone by mixing snake venom in it, then rub it on whatever. When a person touches the surface with the venom, they die but it appears as if they died from a heart attack."

Marian shivered. "Then why didn't they do that, instead of making it apparent that she was murdered?"

Charlie answered. "Too risky, clearly, they wanted Tammy to die, not Peter. And they knew what she was allergic to." He looked at Jack. "Kind of overkill, I'd say."

He nodded, "Yeah, but I'm thinking that maybe they didn't know exactly how she would react." Jack ate another piece of bacon.

"Are you saying they may not have wanted her to die?" Marian was clearly confused.

"No, I think they wanted her to die. Why go to that extent if they only wanted her to suffer a bit?" Charlie drained the last of the coffee from his cup.

Officer Watson interjected as he slathered another piece of toast with jam, "And this was most definitely planned."

"Oh, absolutely!" Charlie rested back in his chair. "Now we have to narrow down the suspects. I say Sophia and Kaye are off the list."

They all agreed.

Charlie held up his fist. "That leaves us with Peter, Antonio, Bella, and Henry." He popped up a finger with each name, wiggling four fingers in the air.

"Surely, Antonio isn't a suspect anymore. I mean, he clearly loved her. Why would he kill her?"

Charlie rubbed his wife's shoulder. "He may have decided if he couldn't have her, no one could."

"But after all these years, why now?"

Charlie shrugged, "Something pushed him over the edge, who knows, maybe the vow renewal ceremony."

"I have my doubts, too. He seems to have a very good alibi, too many witnesses." Officer Watson dusted crumbs from his hands.

"I thought that too, but we don't know when the toothbrush was loaded. But we do know it had to have been the day she died and after Peter left for the bar, it's a tight timeline."

Charlie flipped open his notepad. "According to Peter, they went to dinner at five-thirty and Tammy brushed her teeth before leaving. They arrived back to the suite around nine-fifteen, Peter left for the bar at approximately nine-thirty, leaving Tammy alone and at that time she had not brushed her teeth again."

He looked around the table. "So we can agree that someone could have put the stingers in the toothbrush after five-thirty that night?"

They all agreed.

"But Charlie, that doesn't narrow down the suspects." Marian looked frustrated then brightened. "But we do know for a fact that Bella was in the suite after the Fergusons went to dinner and so was Henry."

"Ah, but where was Antonio? All we know is that he was bartending at ten o'clock. Where was he between five-thirty and ten? And we know he had access to the suite."

Marian crossed her arms against her chest. "So we're back to four suspects."

Jack shot up his hand like a third grader with the right answer. "Oh, but we can say that someone was with Tammy when she died? The bruise on her leg, someone kicked her right as she died."

"Henry?" Marian looked confused. "Of all the people, why him?"

Charlie looked at his notes. "You said she died around eleven, right?"

"Well, yeah, but I can't say exactly when, no way to pinpoint the time."

"Then I think we may be able to rule out Antonio, but I don't want to jump the gun and pin it on Henry. I want to talk with Peter again just to make sure that Bella was with him all the time." Charlie paused. "We also need to make sure that Antonio didn't disappear at any time. We need to find that waitress who said she saw Bella and Peter together. She would be a good witness to corroborate or refute anything Peter, Bella, or Antonio has said."

Doctor Nelson groaned, "More interviews?"

"McClung is a cracking good detective. There'll not be any cock-ups in this investigation. He'll see to that. Isn't that what we want Doctor Nelson?"

The doctor threw up his hands in acceptance.

"Thank you, Watson. I like to have all possible scenarios examined. That's why my arrests result in convictions."

"Splendid! I feel even more confident about solving this mystery. Who shall we bring in first?" Officer Watson pulled a pen and small notepad from his pocket.

Charlie flipped through his pad to find a clean page. "I say let's start with Peter, he'll be the easiest to bring in. I'd like to interview that waitress next, then Antonio, Henry, and lastly, Bella."

"How are we going to approach the interviews? Do you want to do them all today and in this same conference room?"

"No, Watson, I think we should find them and interview them on their own turf. They'll feel more relaxed and just may slip up."

Jack took the last piece of bacon. "Will you need me and the doc for anything?"

"I don't think so. What do you think, Watson?"

"No, as a matter of fact, I was thinking that maybe you and Marian would probably get more out of them than you and I could. You know, with me in uniform and being their superior, they may feel a bit threatened. What do you think?"

"Oh, Charlie, you know he's right, we can do this. I know we can." Marian was practically bouncing in her chair. "Please."

Looking at his wife's pleading blue eyes, Charlie wanted to give her anything she desired but he didn't want her to get hurt. *Maybe if I keep her glued to my hip, she won't be able to get herself into any trouble. I really don't want there to be a next time, twice is already more than enough.*

He cupped her eager face into his hands. "Fine, but you have to promise me you will not leave my side. Understand?"

She grabbed his wrists, tilted his hands palms up, and then kissed each one. "That'll be easy enough to do. I love being glued to you."

Marian blushed deeply as the men around the table gasped and snorted.

Charlie hugged her and said, "That's my girl."

Chapter 23

Bella scurried away from the closed conference door when she heard all the chairs scrape against the floor. They would soon be exiting and looking for her. That was the last thing she needed, to be caught eavesdropping on the men who were investigating her and the man she had fantasized about for years. There would be no way to explain why she was even in the hallway. She should be making up the suites. Why did she let Henry talk her into doing this?

She rounded the corner, down another hallway, then trotted down the stairs, finally making her way to her cart. Smiling, she used one of the pristine-white hand towels on her cart to blot the sweat beading on her temples and upper lip. The thought of almost getting caught and the rush of escaping made her feel alive and excited.

Maybe that's why I love creating chaos. She entered Peter's suite. Yes, just Peter's. The flowers on the dresser, a symbol of faded love, were dead. They were the first thing she dumped into the trash.

Peter had asked Bella to pack away his wife's things. She gathered everything that had belonged to the dead woman, stuffed it all in plastic garbage bags and tossed the bags into the closet. If only the clothes had fit Bella, she would have kept a few of the items. The woman had superb taste in fashion. Bella had hoped to find jewelry lying about but there was nothing.

She must've locked it all away in the safe before she croaked. "Or choked on her own tongue to be more accurate." Bella snorted.

Bella looked at herself in the wide dresser mirror and ran her hands over her voluptuous figure. *That woman was a fat cow compared to me.* Bella refused to even think Tammy's name, much less say it.

She wondered what her mama would think about her being with the man she had once kissed. Bella really didn't care what her mama thought or her grandmother either. She had been suffocated for years by those two bitter old women, but her memories of her daddy brought her comfort. *Why did you have to go, Daddy? I miss you so much.*

Bella looked at her reflection and grinned, quickly forgetting her past. Her hands smoothed down all the fly-away hairs in the French braid wrapped around her head. She was glad that she let the stylist in the spa dye her black hair to a deep rich auburn color. It complimented her perfect complexion.

Looking around the suite, it didn't appear that Peter had slept in the bed. The bed was a little crumpled, but the covers were still in place, and a hand towel had been used, tossed casually on the vanity. Bella's good mood was quickly replaced with a dull anger or was it jealousy? She looked at her watch. Ten o'clock. *Hmm, maybe he got an early start.*

After Detective McClung saw her in Peter's suite last night, Bella decided to avoid Peter the rest of the night. She had no idea if he had spent the night with someone or where he was this morning but nothing was going to stop her plan, and the plan was going better than she had dreamed of. So many years of just waiting.

Bella picked up the empty whisky bottle. Next, she examined the two glasses for lipstick. None visible. *Maybe Peter had a drink with that detective, passed out and then headed to the bar this morning.* It made sense to her. He was already drunk when she confronted him with the picture and with a little more of the expensive whisky, he must have passed out.

The picture. Bella remembered the day she found it and wondered who the man standing next to her mother was. The picture was taken at the restaurant where her mother worked. Bella asked her mother about the handsome man leaning against the bar with his arms crossed protectively over his chest. Her mother said it was just some gentleman who came into the restaurant all the time then suddenly stopped coming.

Bella saw the sad smile on her mother's face and knew he was more than just some gentleman, so she asked her grandmother about it. Her grandmother didn't want to talk about it and told Bella to go ask her mother. When she explained to her grandmother that her mama said it was just some gentleman that came into the restaurant, Bella saw anger flash across her grandmother's wrinkled face. Her grandmother snarled that the man was far from being a gentleman and one day some woman would make him pay. Bella's grandmother clamped her mouth shut, snatched the picture from Bella's hand, wadded the picture into a ball, tossed it on the floor, and then abruptly left the room. The photo was never mentioned again.

Bella straightened up the bathroom. *This is where it happened.* She smiled. She moved on to the bed, smoothed out the spread, and then opened the heavy drapes, letting the sunshine flood the suite, dust particles floating in the stream of light. *Looks like fairy dust.* Bella grinned. She opened the balcony door, stepped out and straightened the furniture Peter had moved when he recoiled from her rage. She chuckled. "God, I'm a good actress."

Taking a deep breath, Bella filled her lungs with sea air, stretched her arms over her head, and then gave herself a tight hug. *All is right with the world. One day, I'll be standing here as a guest, not as a maid.* Dropping her hands to her hips, she strutted around like Yul Brenner in the movie, *The King and I.* "And that day will be soon." She wanted to finish all of her assigned cabins quickly, so she could find Peter and continue with her plan. But she first had to report to Henry, tell him another round of questions were coming.

Bella stepped inside the suite. A sparkle, in between the nightstand and bed, caught her eye. Bella moved the small stand away from the king-sized bed. A pair of diamond studs. Bella laughed as she picked them up, dropping the earrings into her pocket. "Payday, Peter, payday."

Chapter 24

"Did you hear that?" Marian poked her head out of the conference room door.

"What? Charlie looked over her shoulder.

She shook her head after seeing the corridor empty. "Nothing I guess. Sounded like someone running down the hallway but there's no one in sight." Marian shrugged, "Oh, well."

"What do you say we go back to the cabin, freshen up, and then stroll around the ship before we start our snooping? Just some you and me time, time well spent." Charlie wiggled his eyebrows mischievously.

Marian slipped her arm around her husband's waist as they walked down the hallway toward the stairs. "Mmm, sounds like a plan to me. We can burn off a few calories."

"Will you two please save your double-entendres for when no one is within earshot? Sheesh!" Jack put his hands over his ears.

"Jack, what on Earth are you talking about? Marian laughed. "I thought I was the only one in this group who eavesdropped."

Officer Watson and Doctor Nelson chuckled.

"Apparently, we all do."

Charlie pulled Marian aside to let the three men pass by. "Watson, I'll give you a ring to let you know what we find out."

As Watson passed by, he said, "I'll await breathlessly."

The men laughed boisterously.

"You guys are terrible." Marian slapped playfully at the men clutching their sides. "Charlie, you're no better."

Charlie wiped away a tear. "I'm sorry love." He grabbed her. "Let's give 'em something to talk about." He kissed her deeply.

"All right, you've proved your point, go to your cabin. We've seen enough." Doctor Nelson shook his head, "Children!"

"Ah, it's good to have a belly laugh every now then, my friends." Officer Watson clamped his hands on Jack's and Doctor Nelson's shoulders as he walked between them.

Charlie and Marian watched them disappear as they turned the corner toward the elevator bank.

"Finally, alone at last." Charlie pinched Marian's chin. "Now how about burning some calories, shall we?"

"Let's."

As they made their way toward the stairs, Marian leaned her head on Charlie. "I know I heard someone running down the hallway. Someone was listening to us."

"Yeah, I know. The door was closed when we sat down to breakfast but was open just a sliver when we finished. I didn't hear it when it opened." He leaned his cheek against her head. "Did you?"

"No."

"It had to be one of the suspects but they didn't hear anything that they probably don't know already." Charlie paused, "No, that's not completely true. Depending on when they started to listen, they may have learned the truth about Antonio and Tammy."

Marian separated from Charlie when they reached the staircase and held onto the rail. "Well, they were bound to find out after the investigation."

"Yeah. Enough talk about that. It's us time, now."

She sighed, "Sounds good." Glancing up the stairwell, Marian caught a glimpse of someone jumping back out of sight. She smirked and thought, *just a shadow, that's all, just a shadow.*

Charlie opened the door to their suite, ushered Marian inside and shut the door. "Oops, can't forget this." He took the 'Do Not Disturb' card, and as he opened the door to hang it on the door handle, he caught a glimpse of Henry and Bella entering a suite down and across the hallway. *Nope, I got something better to do inside my cabin than to worry about what those two are doing.*

He hung the card, shut the door, locked it, and then turned his attention to Marian who needed help unzipping her pretty little sundress. *Yep, this is definitely more interesting.* "Here, let me help you with that.

Chapter 25

"What do you mean there are going to be more interviews? Why?" Henry was not happy, not at all happy.

Bella had found Henry delivering flowers to one of the suites and followed him inside the empty cabin. "I don't know. I got there right before the meeting broke up."

"You should have told me sooner."

"I told you as soon as I found out."

"Did you hear anything else besides more interviews?

"All I know is that detective and his wife are going to do the questioning and they will be talking with you, me, Antonio, Peter, and Shannon."

"Shannon?"

"You know her, the new girl from Scotland works in the Stargazer most nights."

Henry frowned.

"Yes, you do, bright red hair, blue eyes, freckles across her nose, a heavy accent that seems to turn on the men."

"Oh, the one with the loud laugh."

"That's the one."

"Why talk to her?'

Bella rolled her eyes. "She was working at the Stargazer that night. She saw me and Peter together."

Henry pulled a brown leaf from one of the stems in the arrangement. "I do not understand why they need to speak with me again." He turned and looked at Bella. "I told them everything. What else do they want? Besides, Antonio is the one who said he found her dead."

A chill ran up Bella's spine. The look on Henry's face was disturbing. She often wondered what thoughts crept around in his head. "You're right." Her nose and forehead crinkled together, "Come to think of it, why was he even in their cabin so late at night?"

Henry smacked the top of Bella's head. "Exactly! He is the one they should be focusing on. Think about it. Why do you think he was there?"

She rubbed the top of her head, then the reason suddenly popped into her head. "No, really?" Bella shook her head. "I can't believe Miss Prim and Proper was carrying on with Antonio."

Henry shrugged, "Believe what you will but looks can be deceiving." He stared at Bella to prove his point.

She gritted her teeth. "Well, you're one to be throwing stones."

Henry grabbed her arm.

"Let go of me, now."

He held fast onto her arm, pulling her close, almost nose to nose. "Look, we cannot be turning against each other. Remember, we are on their list, even though it is clear to us that Antonio is obviously the one who did it, people lie to save their own necks or for revenge. Who knows what Shannon and Antonio will say?"

Bella felt her stomach churn. *Revenge*. She licked her dry lips, worried about the people on board she had crossed. *Revenge*. Not a good word when you're on the receiving end.

Chapter 26

Charlie lay on the bed, his hands behind his head, and a smile on his face. He listened to the shower running and Marian's sweet voice singing, *In My Life*. He closed his eyes and said a silent prayer of thanks to God for granting him the patience to wait for true love. How much would he have missed if he had just settled?

In his eyes, Marian was everything he had ever wanted. She had blossomed since they first met over three months ago, from a tiny bud into a prize rose. She was relaxed, happy, and alive. Charlie knew it was love that transformed her and it delighted him knowing it was the love they shared for each other.

The water stopped, he knew it would only be about twenty minutes and she would be ready to hit the ground running. She was a natural beauty and didn't need all the paint his ex-girlfriend, Holly needed.

Holly was a good girl but there was just that … that something missing. Their relationship just seemed to dissolve, disappeared gradually, no goodbyes, as if they both knew it was wrong, it died a painless, silent death.

Death. Why did someone kill Tammy? Charlie ran through the suspects and possible reasons. It had to be jealousy, but was it jealousy over Peter or Tammy? And why kill Tammy in that manner, to make her suffer so much? Or maybe it was revenge? If so, what had Tammy done to cause such animosity? And it was planned. For someone to go to the lengths of finding out her allergies, mixing peanut oil in DMSO, putting it into the toothpaste and on the toothbrush, collecting honey bee stingers, and then planting them in Tammy's toothbrush, was nothing more than cold-blooded, premeditated murder. No question about it. He had it narrowed down to two people but couldn't quite decide on the motive.

Marian stood at the foot of the bed, interrupting his contemplation, a thick bathrobe was loosely tied around her waist.

"I'll be ready to go in about five minutes."

"Hmm, I see someone poking out there that needs some lovin.'"

"What?"

Charlie pointed to her robe hanging open, partially exposing her chest.

She laughed and cinched her robe closed. "Go get ready. You promised me a stroll and a day of interrogations."

"My, you are a cheap date."

"Oh, yeah! Be forewarned, you'll pay later, my dearest darling." She jumped on the bed, laid beside him and threw an arm across his chest. "But I think you'll like it."

Charlie rolled over, pinning her to the bed. "I'd like to pay now if you don't mind."

Marian playfully beat on his chest. "No. Stroll, interrogations, dinner, and only then can you settle your debt."

Charlie kissed the tip of her nose. "As you wish." He jumped off the bed, went into the bathroom, and then jumped into the shower. He smiled hearing Marian banging around in the cabin. It brought back memories of the first time he was in her house. She clanked around pots and pans, having no concept of the noise she was creating.

Charlie toweled off and went into the cabin. Marian was dressed and out on the balcony, lying on the chaise, her face sheltered under a big straw hat to keep the wrinkles at bay. He dressed quickly and then joined her on the balcony. Standing at the foot of her lounger, he squatted down and squeezed her bare feet. "My ageless wonder, ready to go?"

"Yep, all I need are my sandals." She leaned forward, grabbed her ankles, eye to eye with Charlie. "I love you. Just thought you should know that."

He held her hands and helped her to stand. "Of course you do and don't ever forget that."

"Me? Never. Now let's stroll and discuss our plan of action."

♣

As they walked down the hallway toward the promenade deck, Charlie hooked his arm around Marian's. "So, what is your plan of action?"

"Follow your lead."

"Seriously, that's all you have?"

Marian laughed. "Well, not exactly, I thought I'd listen as you grill them and interrupt if I think of something."

Charlie grunted.

"I'll warn you first by rubbing your arm or maybe your ankle with my foot." Marian stopped. "Did you see that?"

Charlie looked in the direction Marian was staring. There was nothing there. Just sunlight filtering through the round window in the heavy wooden door that led to the promenade deck. "What did you see?" He felt a cold finger run down his spine. This was the second time Marian thought she had seen something or someone. He hoped it wasn't danger lurking around the corner, waiting to fall upon Marian. *Not, again, please, not again.*

She swallowed and shook her head. "Nothing. I guess it was just a shadow." Marian continued toward the door. "Let's do one turn around the deck and then go to the pool bar. That's probably where we'll find Peter at this time of day."

"Okay," Charlie agreed. He pushed open the door, stepped out first, and looked around, holding Marian behind him, just in case there was someone lying in wait, but there was nothing menacing in sight.

He held his wife's hand as they strolled down the deck, keeping a watchful eye. "I have it narrowed down to two suspects." He tapped his temple. "Though I'm a bit thick when it comes to the motive."

"Tell me, who do you think it is?"

"Nope. I don't want to muddle your suspicions. But," He held up his index finger, "I'd like your help with the motive."

"Okay."

"Being a woman, and you're very much a woman I may add," Charlie kissed her hand, "and I thank you very much. But back to the point. Why would you kill Tammy?"

With a heavy sigh, Marian began to think aloud. "If I were the criminal kind, if she stole you away from me, I'd have murder in mind. Although, if that happened, I'm not so sure if I'd kill her or you." She looked at Charlie. "Maybe both, so beware."

"Never would happen. Why settle for less when I have the best?"

"Good answer. You shall live for another day. Now if she killed you, there'd be hell to pay."

"Thank you."

"Think nothing of it. Now, if I was really vindictive, I may kill her if she embarrassed me, I mean really embarrassed me."

"Like how?"

Marian scratched the back of her head. "Oh, I don't know. If she blurted out loud on purpose something about my past that I didn't want to be known, like being in jail."

Charlie stopped and looked her, "Have you?"

"Pff! I've never even had a traffic ticket." As she began to walk, she asked, "Have you ever been in jail?"

"I've been in many a jail but I personally have never been thrown inside of a cell."

"That's good to know. Why would you have killed Tammy?"

Charlie rubbed his chin. "Probably the same reasons as you. Maybe revenge for something she did to my family. Or just plain hated her."

"I guess we'll just have to find out who did it to know why."

"Uhuh. We've finished one turn, now we have to go up top. Walk or ride?"

Marian was tired, not enough sleep. "Let's ride, my feet hurt and I need to cool off. Let's take the glass elevators."

"As you wish."

Marian smiled, content with her life.

Charlie was thankful they were the only ones in their elevator. As it went up slowly, he circled his arms around his wife, resting his chin on her head, and wished they could have at least one day without this blasted investigation looming over them.

The doors slid open and they made their way down a short hallway toward the pool. Sliding glass doors opened automatically as they approached the pool area. A blast of hot air, sounds of laughter, reggae music, and smoke from chicken and hamburgers being cooked on the outdoor grills welcomed them as they stepped outside.

Charlie pointed to the opposite side of the pool. There sat Peter, alone. They walked past sweating bodies being roasted by the Caribbean sun, smells of coconut and shea butter were caught in the breeze.

"Peter, mind if we join you?" Charlie lightly touched Peter's shoulder.

Peter grunted, "Depends. Are you here to cheer me up or interrogate me again?"

"I'll be honest with you. I have two questions, then we'll leave you alone if that's what you want. Or after you answer our questions, Marian and I will help cheer you up. It's your call."

Peter stared at a tall sweating glass setting before him. With a dark blue straw, he slowly swirled the clear liquid, the ice made a tinkling sound. "I don't mind, ask your questions." His shoulders sagged.

"What are you drinking? Is it good?" With Charlie's help, Marian hopped up on the tall bar stool.

"Water."

Marian looked over her shoulder at Charlie, surprised it was just water.

Charlie motioned to the bartender for two more glasses of water. He sat next to Marian so Peter wouldn't have to swivel his head side-to-side when they spoke to him.

"Peter, I'll make this quick. Was Bella with you the whole time you were in the bar?"

"No, she appeared around ten o'clock or so, then disappeared on and off until around midnight." Peter looked at his watch, motioned for the bartender, "A Bloody Mary, no salt, no ice in the glass, please," he looked at Marian, "Would you like one? That guy makes the best I've ever had." He pointed to the grinning man. "Charlie, want one? I'm buying."

"No, thank you, I'll stick with water for now. What about you, Marian?"

"Sure, I'd love to try one."

Peter held up two fingers for the bartender. "And before you ask Charlie, I have no idea where Bella disappeared to. Sometimes, she'd be gone for a few minutes and sometimes longer, maybe fifteen minutes or so. I was drunk so time really meant nothing to me. She didn't say where she went, and I didn't care enough to ask."

"Did Bella ever drink?" Marian thanked the bartender as he set down the tall narrow glass with a thick stalk of celery for a stirrer and two olives speared on a blue plastic sword to complete the garnish.

"Nope. Never saw a drink in her hand. Maybe that's what she was doing when she disappeared but then again, I never smelled anything on her breath, either."

"Did you see Henry or Antonio in the bar?" Charlie took a tiny sip of Marian's drink just to verify to himself that he still loathed tomato juice, and then quickly washed away the vile taste from his mouth with a huge gulp of water.

"Yes, both of them. Henry stopped by, pulled Bella to the side for what appeared to be a mildly heated discussion. I don't know what they said. I went to the bar for a bottle of Aberfeldy. I'd figured a bottle was more cost effective than the shots I'd been ordering. That's when I saw Antonio for the first time that night, behind the bar doing something, then he disappeared into the back room. I'm pretty sure he didn't see me. The next time I saw him was when he was yelling at me about Tammy."

Peter stared straight ahead, cradling his drink, a minuscule tear clung to the corner of his eye. "For some reason right after you guys left last night, it hit me that my wife is dead. She's really dead. Tammy's gone and she's never coming back."

He flicked away the tear threatening to drip down his cheek and chuckled, "Maybe, it's being back in our suite." Peter rubbed his nose.

"This morning, I saw Tammy's book lying on the end table waiting for her." He sighed, opened his mouth to speak but nothing came out.

Marian squeezed his forearm. "I'm sorry. I want you to know that I've been where you are now."

Peter chuckled sarcastically, "Really? You've been there." He shook his head.

"My first husband of nineteen years was killed in a plane crash eleven years ago. So, yes, I know how it feels." Marian was able to confess without crying. She felt Charlie's strong arm around her waist, his breath on her neck as he rested his chin on her shoulder and pressed his head against hers.

Peter covered her hand with his. "I'm sorry. I didn't know."

The trio sat in silence for a few minutes.

"Marian, maybe we should leave Peter alone."

Marian started to wiggle off the high barstool.

Peter held onto her hand. "Please, don't go. I need to talk to someone." He looked at Marian and Charlie. "Please stay."

"All right, let me get us some lunch. Peter, would you like something to eat?"

"I'm not hungry but I know I should eat something." Peter started to stand.

"No, you and Marian stay and chat. I'll get you something."

Peter didn't argue. "Just a hamburger, lettuce, tomato, and cheese."

Charlie stood, ready to take Marian's order. "Marian, what would you like for me to get you?"

"A hotdog, mustard, ketchup, and relish, if they have it." She kissed his cheek. "Thank you."

"You've got yourself a fine man."

Marian smiled. "Yes, I know. He's practically perfect."

"Yeah." Peter finished his Bloody Mary in silence.

In between the bottles of alcohol on the shelves, Marian watched Peter's reflection in the bar's mirror. *If he killed Tammy, the man is one mighty fine actor.* Marian sipped her drink, feeling the effects of the bartender's heavy-hand with the vodka. She looked around for Charlie and saw him heading their way, holding two plates, one piled high with food. *I hope we're sharing that one.* Her stomach growled.

Charlie slid a plate with a hamburger, fries, and three cookies: oatmeal raisin, chocolate chip, and plain chocolate, in front of Peter. "I know you said just a hamburger, but you can't have a hamburger without fries and the cookies were too tempting."

"I'll eat the cookies if you don't," Marian chimed in.

"There's plenty on our plate, Marian, leave the man's cookies alone."

"Oh, sorry," she giggled and grabbed a chocolate one off of their plate.

The bartender gave them fresh glasses of water. "Would you like anything else besides water?"

Charlie and Marian shook their heads.

"I'll have a Coke with a splash of Jack." Peter held up his thumb and index about a quarter-inch apart.

"Charlie, I was telling Marian what a fine man you are. Believe it or not, she agreed."

Marian leaned over, giving Charlie a quick peck.

"Mm, chocolatey." Charlie licked his lips.

"I wasn't a good husband, not at all." Peter bit a fry in half, tossed the other half onto his plate. "She was a good wife, though. No complaints."

He took a sip of the Coke the bartender just handed him. "Do you think she was having an affair with that concierge? Peter smirked, "I guess you would know for a fact. You did question him, right?"

"Yes, do you really want to know the answer? Think about it before you answer." Charlie squirted mustard on the side of their plate and then ran a couple of fries through it.

Peter rubbed the back of his neck. "I already know the answer. For Christ's sake, he was always our concierge. It was staring me right in the face. And I thought I was the cagey one. What a brilliant disguise they had."

Charlie and Marian ate in silence, letting Peter spill out his thoughts.

"I can't be mad at her, I mean, look at all I did to her, always searching for the next chippie. At least she had the decency to stick to one man." Peter scratched his chin. "I guess she did, now, I don't know."

He looked at Charlie. "What am I supposed to think about my wife?"

"Think the best of her, she stuck around for thirty-five years, and you said she was a good wife. Tammy was very discreet, protected your feelings, and not only her reputation but yours as well."

Charlie watched Peter push around his fries. He wished he could read Peter's thoughts. *You never really know a person, their thoughts and secrets. Never.* He rubbed Marian's back and she leaned over, shoulder to shoulder. *I won't ever have to wonder about her. If it were left up to her, she'd be attached to my hip.*

Peter finished the Coke, motioned for another one. "I should have met you two years ago, maybe none of this would have happened."

"What do you mean?" Charlie wondered if Peter was going to reveal more about that night.

"Maybe your happy marriage would've influenced me. Maybe I wouldn't have treated Tammy so badly. Yeah, I treated her like a forgotten goldfish, gave her a house to live in, and then tossed her a few crumbs of affection every now and then." Peter picked out the raisins from the cookie and ate them one by one. "I didn't kill her. I swear I didn't."

Charlie decided since Peter brought up the subject, he'd run with it. "Who do you think did? Out of all the people on this ship, who do you think would have wanted her dead?"

"I've thought about that. At first, I had no clue. But maybe Bella did it. Now that I know about her mother, even though there was nothing between us, maybe Bella thinks there was. Maybe she killed Tammy to avenge her mother's broken heart. I don't know." Peter ate the raisin-less cookie. "The girl seems a bit squirrely to me."

"Is it possible that Bella wants to take Tammy's place?"

Peter shrugged. "No one can take Tammy's place. Bella can want all she wants to but it's not gonna happen. She's a silly girl, all right to have fun with, but not someone I'd want to spend the rest of my life with." He sniffed loudly and wiped his nose with a paper napkin.

Charlie didn't want Peter to dwell on his loss, afraid he'd shut down in his grief. He needed more facts to find the murderer. "Getting back to Bella's mother, tell me exactly what happened there, the details could shed light on Bella's motive." Charlie took out his pad and pen.

"That was a long time ago, I'd forgotten about Bella's mother. To be perfectly honest, I don't remember most of the women I meet. But I'll answer your question the best I can. She worked at a bar-restaurant type of joint. Good food as best as I can remember. There were, I think, three waitresses there that I spent time with, just whoever was available at the moment."

"One more than another?"

"Not that I remember, but Bella's mother and one other one, started to get a little too clingy for comfort. I stopped going to the restaurant because of that."

Marian interrupted, "I'm sorry but did you have sex with any of them?"

Charlie had to press his lips together to keep from laughing and decided to see how far Marian would go with her line of questioning.

Peter pulled his head back in surprise, surprised a lady would ask such a blatant question. "Well, uh, no, not all of them."

"Bella's mother and the other clingy one?"

"I don't feel uncomfortable discussing my sex life with you. Him, but not you." Peter pointed to Charlie and then motioned for the bartender to bring him another drink.

Marian felt the heat from a hot flash, and Charlie gripped her forearm.

"I think what my wife is getting at, is maybe one of the women may have thought your relationship was more than casual. Do you remember one of them saying such?"

"Yeah, that's why I stopped going to the restaurant. But I always make it perfectly clear to whoever it was at the time that I was married and intended to stay that way."

The bartender set down the fresh drink in front of Peter, who pressed the cold glass to his cheek and neck.

"What was said to spook you?" Charlie was beginning to think this was the piece he'd been missing.

"Both said their husbands were out of the picture and maybe we could take it a step further. I don't know if they meant marriage or me setting them up as my mistress. I didn't care at the time, I just vanished."

Charlie tugged his earlobe. *No closer to the truth.* "Do you remember either one of them talking about their children?"

"Nope." Peter took a long drink. "I didn't care about their lives; it was all about having a good time. Only found out that Bella's mother had a kid from another waitress."

What a pig, Charlie thought. He could just imagine what Marian must be thinking. And with that thought, Marian chimed in.

"Why on earth did you get married?"

Peter shook his head. "You don't hold any punches do you?"

Marian blushed.

"But I'll answer your question. I know a good thing when I see it and Tammy was the best thing I'd ever seen."

"Humph, so why did you chase other women if she was the best thing you'd ever seen?"

Peter tilted his head. "I don't know, the thrill, the conquest. It made me feel … I don't know … powerful."

"Did Tammy think you were powerful?" Marian took a big gulp of water to stifle her anger burning inside.

Marian's words hit Peter hard. His countenance fell, making him look ten years older. "She read a lot of books, the ones with half-naked men on the covers. I guess when that wasn't enough, she turned to Antonio." He chuckled sadly. "In reality, I didn't have the power to keep even one woman happy."

Chapter 27

"Was I too mean?" Marian didn't like being rude or hateful but someone being nonchalant about infidelity was more than she could tolerate.

Charlie had his arm draped over his wife's shoulders as they walked into Officer Watson's office. "No, sometimes the truth can be brutal. It can make people realize just how insignificant they are to other people."

"Maybe I should go back to our cabin and read."

Turning her to face him, Charlie tilted up her chin so he could look straight into her eyes. "Is that what you really want to do?"

Marian bit her bottom lip as she thought about his question. *Read or ask questions. Hmm, they both sound good. Relax or maybe solve a murder.* She made up her mind. "No, I'd rather be with you."

"All right, let's check-in with Watson to see when and where Shannon Thompson is scheduled to work."

Charlie knocked on Watson's office door.

"Enter," Officer Watson granted them permission.

When they entered his office, Watson was staring over his half-rimmed glasses in their directions. His face split into a happy grin. "Come on in, take a seat, and tell me what you've learned."

"Not much, but we can rule out Peter. I'd like to speak with Shannon Thompson next. Do you have her schedule?"

Officer Watson quickly pulled out a sheet of paper from one of the dozen multi-colored folders stacked neatly on the corner of his desk. He scanned the paper, and then glanced at the oversized clock hanging over the door. "Crikey! I didn't realize it was so late. She's on duty now, a twelve-hour shift it appears, and she's in the Stargazer lounge."

"How will I know her?"

"Ah, you can't miss her." Watson pulled out another sheet of paper and handed it to Charlie. "Look for the girl with flaming red hair."

Charlie and Marian studied the picture Shannon had taken for her work ID.

"Oh, she's a pretty girl. Look at those blue eyes."

"She's attractive but she doesn't come close to your beauty, no one does." Charlie glanced back to Shannon's employment details. "So, she's been onboard for less than four months?"

Officer Watson took the paper that Charlie handed him. "Yes, this is her first tour of duty on a cruise ship. And from what I understand, she's doing a cracking good job."

"Fancy a cocktail?" Charlie stood, offering his hand to Marian.

"Yes, I've heard of a drink called a Mojito. I'd like to try one."

Charlie held up his elbow. "Shall we?"

"Let's." Marian threaded her arm around his. "Care to join us, Officer Watson?"

He patted a different, higher stack of folders. "I'd love to but duty calls. My fingers are crossed, we can get this murder put to bed soon."

"Consider it done." With just a few more pieces, the puzzle would be complete, Charlie was confident he would have them soon, very soon.

Officer Watson held up both of his hands with his fingers crossed. "Cheers!"

♣

As soon as they entered the sparsely populated bar, Charlie saw Shannon, her red hair was like a flame in the dark. He walked over to the bar. "May I speak with the supervisor?"

"You're lookin' at em mate. What can I do ya for?" The dirty blonde hair, tan, hunky Joe answered Charlie but smiled at Marian who clung even tighter to Charlie's arm.

Charlie had a strong dislike for men like the one behind the bar. "My name is Detective Charlie McClung. I see you admire my lady friend, so let me introduce you to my wife, Marian, and I didn't catch your name, mate."

The young man's smile faltered and he quickly turned his attention away from Marian. "My name's Bruce. A pleasure to meet ya, sir and ya missus."

"Thank you. I need to speak with Shannon Thompson for a few minutes if that is okay with you."

"Go right ahead, sir."

Charlie paused, "Before I do, let me ask you a question, did Antonio Caruso fill in for you a few nights ago?"

"Yes, sir, I ate somethin' that didn't quite agree with me. Feel much better now. Antonio is a fine bloke."

"Thank you." Charlie turned away and scanned the room for Shannon. He found her chatting with a few customers.

"Excuse me, so sorry to interrupt."

Shannon replied with a generous smile, "No problem, what can I get you?"

"I'd like a Mojito," Marian ordered eagerly.

"And for you sir?'

"May we take that table over in the far corner?" Charlie pointed to a deserted section of the bar.

"Sure thing, sit anywhere you like. Is there something I can get for you?" Shannon followed them to a table next to a wall of windows.

"Uh, I'd like a Diet Dr Pepper and a glass of water for now. But before you go, my name is Detective Charlie McClung. I need to ask you a few questions."

Still smiling, Shannon asked, "Why do you want to question me?"

"I'm sure you heard about the death of one of the guests."

"Yes, but what does that have to do with me?"

"You were serving the dead woman's husband drinks the night she died."

"Oh, dear! Who?"

"Charlie, do you mind if she gets our drinks before you start the questions?" Marian fluttered her eyelashes at him.

He laughed. "Sure, my wife is craving a Mojito, never had one before."

Shannon's smile remained as she replied, "Mojito, a Diet Dr Pepper, and a glass of water." She sashayed away.

Marian grinned sheepishly, "Sorry, but I'm really thirsty."

It didn't take long for the striking redhead to return with a full tray.

"Ah, here she comes with your drink. That was quick, now you won't die from thirst."

Marian swatted playfully at his shoulder.

Shannon sat three tall glasses on the table and looked around to see if any customers needed to be served while she waited for Charlie to sign the receipt, charging the drinks to their suite. Everyone looked taken care of, so she turned her full attention to Charlie. "Shall I sit down?"

"Please, but it shouldn't take long, only a few questions."

"Aye then, do you mind if I sit facin' the room, just in case someone's in need of a drink?" Shannon was already pulling out a chair close to the wall of windows.

Charlie took out his pad. "When does your shift normally start?"

"My shift starts at noon and ends at midnight."

"Are those your normal hours?"

"Aye, that's a fact."

Charlie smiled at her lovely Scottish accent. "Do you remember seeing Antonio that night?"

"Aye, Bruce," she pointed to the bartender, "ate somethin' that had him spendin' a bit too much time in the lavy, so he called Antonio to cover for him at the last minute. You can always count on Antonio."

"What time did Antonio take over?"

Shannon did a quick scan of the room to make sure all of the patrons were okay. "Mmm, I'd say around ten o'clock, give or take a minute or two. He was supposed to end his shift at midnight but Bella was too busy carousin' with some man."

"Yeah, can you tell me about the man?" Charlie was encouraged by Shannon's details.

She shrugged. "Older American, average looks and build, nothin' to get excited about. He must have been rich for Bella to be hangin' onto his every word."

"You've never seen him before?"

"Yes, I've seen once or twice sittin' at the bar alone."

Charlie heard the ice clink in Marian's glass. So did Shannon, she jumped up. "Would you like another?"

Marian looked at Charlie and gave him a lopsided grin. "Should I?"

She's tipsy. He chuckled. "It must have been good."

Marian bobbed her head, still wearing the lopsided grin. "Yep."

Charlie nodded at Shannon. "Bring her another one." And he gave Marian a squeeze. "It's our honeymoon."

"Congratulations!" Shannon picked up the empty glass and looked at Charlie's barely touched glasses. "Would you like somethin' else?"

"Thank you, no, but could you get her something to eat, like a few crackers and some cheese, anything like that would be good." Charlie felt Marian lean heavily on him as her arm curled around his waist.

Shannon saw a man across the room hold up his empty glass and she held up her hand in acknowledgment. "Do you mind?"

Charlie motioned for her to take care of her customers.

"Looks like rum goes straight to your little peanut head."

"Yeah, I thought I ate enough at lunch to stave off the effects of alcohol. Who knew?" Marian lightly slapped her forehead. "Whoa, shouldn't have done that. Made me dizzy," she giggled.

"By the way, Charlie, you're asking good questions. You're a great cop, you know that." She rested her chin on his shoulder. "I love you."

Charlie laughed and patted her cheek. "Of course you do, dear."

Shannon returned with a tray of assorted crackers, cheeses, fruits, nuts, cold cuts, a glass of water, and a Mojito. "Here you go. Is this what you had in mind for your bride?"

"Oh, yum!" Marian picked up the Mojito.

Charlie stayed her hand. "Try eating something first." He looked to Shannon, "Thank you, this is perfect. When you finish with the other customers, I still have a few more questions."

"No problem, be back in a jiffy."

Charlie watched Shannon interact with the other people. He saw her keep looking around the room to make sure no one was ignored. She was fast and alert.

Shannon returned in a matter of minutes.

"Whew, I should be free for a few, if no else comes in." The waitress sat down, looking at the platter of snacks. Shannon grinned; most of the nuts were eaten, as was the fruit.

"I'll try to make this quick, I see it's getting busier." Charlie flipped his notepad to a clean page. "Did Antonio act strange or leave the bar for any length of time?"

"He got upset when Bella didn't show up on time and the only time I didn't see him at the bar was when he went in the back to get a bottle of wine for Henry. That's it." Shannon continued to scan the room.

"What about Henry, did he act strange?"

Shannon screwed up her face. "Well, I don't know Henry that well, keeps to himself, but he sure didn't like Bella bein' with that American." Her eyes got big. "Say, is he the dead lady's husband?"

"Yes." Charlie waited for her reaction.

"Holy mother! I heard that there was a scene in the bar after I went off shift. So it was the American that Antonio yelled at." Shannon shook her head slowly.

"Back to Henry, what did he do to make you think he wasn't happy with Bella?" Charlie hoped she would confirm what Peter had said.

Shannon didn't hesitate, "I was takin' a drink order from the table next to the American's table. That one way over there." She pointed to table on the opposite side of the room in a far corner, barely visible. "Henry came over and said somethin' to Bella. She got up and they walked away. The American went to the bar. The music was loud so I didn't hear anythin' they said but I could tell from her hand gestures and the scowl he gave her that he was none too happy with her."

Charlie nodded as he made notes. "Do you know if Bella left the bar at any time or was she with the American the whole time?"

"She disappeared off and on, the lavy I suppose." Shannon cocked her head to one side, "But come to think of it, she was gone an awfully long time after Henry left her." She shook her head. "Can't say for sure how long but it was more than a few minutes. I went to the bar and the American was there. I gave him a bottle of Aberfeldy."

Nodding, she added, "Henry walked up about the time the American left and Antonio returned with the bottle of wine he had ordered. I took the drinks to the table next to the American. He was alone and Bella was nowhere in sight."

Charlie tapped his pen on the pad, deciding if he had any more questions. Shannon had confirmed Peter's statement and revealed a few more interesting facts.

"Shannon, you aren't friends with Bella are you?" Marian asked.

"No, but it's not like we're enemies either. I don't really know her but I've heard rumors, don't know if they're true, what I've seen I would tend to believe them but just to be on the safe side, I decided to steer clear of her."

Charlie took over the questioning. "What kind of rumors?"

"Don't know if I should be repeatin' them, you know, not knowin' if they're truth."

Charlie took a sip of his Diet Dr Pepper. "Well, I can understand that, but sometimes there's a wee bit of truth in rumors."

"Don't worry, Shannon, Charlie's a great keeper of secrets." Marian patted the young girl's hand.

Shannon considered their words. "Well, the one I keep hearin' is that Bella is on the hunt for a rich American. That's all I know about it." She paused, and then gasped, "Say, you don't think it was Bella—"

Charlie cut off her sentence. "We don't know, that's why we're gathering the facts. I know you're very principled, so I don't have to tell you not to say anything to anybody about what was discussed here, right?"

"No, sir, mum's the word." Shannon placed her pale hand over her heart.

Charlie tore a page from his notepad, wrote down his name and cabin number, then gave it to Shannon. "If you think of anything else, or if you see or hear anything that sounds fishy, please contact me."

She tucked the paper into her shirt pocket and darted her eyes toward a man motioning for her attention. "Is that it?"

Charlie saw the customer and stood. "Yes, thank you for taking the time to speak with us. You've been a tremendous help."

"Before I dash off, do either of you need anythin'?" Shannon noticed Marian was nursing the Mojito; the glass was three-quarters full and there were a few bits of cheese and crackers on the platter.

"We're fine, go wait on your other customers. Thank you again for your help." Charlie shook her hand and she went off to wait on her customers.

Marian held a chunk of cheese to her mouth. "She has the prettiest blue eyes. Such a lovely young girl." She popped the cheese into her mouth.

"Yes, but not as beautiful as yours and she may be lovely, but you're a real show stopper."

"Thank you!" She picked through the remaining cheese and selected another piece. "I hope you still say sweet things like that after the honeymoon wears off."

"Ah, now, you hurt me, hurt me bad. The honeymoon will never wear off." Charlie held his wife's pretty face between his hands and kissed her tenderly.

When Charlie released his kiss, Marian snuggled in close. "I'm glad I was sitting down, my knees went weak."

Charlie squeezed her knee. "Should I carry you back to the room?"

"Yes, but after I finish my drink." Marian slowly sipped from her glass. "I've been thinking. I really don't see a need to question Antonio again, do you?"

"No, I agree. Shannon seems to confirm everything he and Peter have said. It's Bella and Henry that seem to be the cagey ones."

Charlie felt Marian stiffen. "What's the matter?"

"Look over there," Marian tilted her head slightly toward the dark corner where Peter and Bella had sat that night. "I think someone is watching us."

Charlie saw a shadow hunker down. He jumped up and hurriedly made his way to the secluded spot. The chair was empty. He felt the seat; it was still warm. *The only way they could have left without being seen is through that door.*

He pushed it opened into a narrow hallway, restrooms on one side, and another door at the other end. He sprinted to the door on the opposite side, pushed it open and walked into the cigar room which led to a smaller bar that opened up to the wide Photo Center hallway. Dozens of people filled the hallway in search of their pictures taken with the ship's mascots and from around the ship's pool, bars, and restaurants. *Damn, lost them.*

He turned and retraced his steps back to the table to see if the person had left behind any clues. There were the remnants of a napkin that had been torn to pieces. Taking a closer look at the paper remains, he noticed they were formed into a shape of a heart but the halves were not joined and were misaligned, one-half being lower the other.

"What the …" Charlie muttered to himself. His head jerked toward Marian. A sigh of relief rushed from his mouth. She was still sitting there waiting for him to return. She was unharmed.

But for how long? Is it her or me or both of us they're stalking? And who could it be? Charlie's heart was beating in time with his racing thoughts as he walked back to Marian.

She stood and fell into his arms, buried her face into his neck and shoulder, feeling safe and protected. "Did you see them? Who was it?"

"No, I didn't see who it was." He swallowed the lump that had formed in his throat and then kissed the top of her head.

"I did see someone, didn't I?" She was on the verge of tears.

"I wish I could say no, but there was definitely someone there. They slipped away before I could get to them."

Marian hugged him tighter. "I'm scared, Charlie."

"No need to be scared. I won't let anything happen to you." I've always been there, right?"

Marian nodded.

"So, you stick with me and no one will harm you." Charlie pulled her into his arms. "You're safe with me."

"I love you so much."

Marian squeezed her eyes together tightly, a tear eased from each corner. "Can we go back to our cabin?"

"As you wish."

Chapter 28

Charlie and Marian sat in a shady spot on their balcony. He was wearing an Atlanta Braves ball cap and Ray-Bans while she sported a floppy straw hat and her Hepburn-like sunglasses. The empty Mojito glass sat on a small, white, wicker table next to Marian with a half-full glass of tepid water and a watered down Diet Dr Pepper.

Both were silent as they reclined on thick padded loungers, the warm Caribbean breezes toyed with the floppy brim of Marian's hat. She reached across the small table and rubbed Charlie's large bicep.

"A penny for your thoughts."

Charlie smiled. "I'm not sure they're worth that much." He sat up, throwing his legs over the side of his chair to face his wife, forearms resting on his thighs, letting his hand dangle between his knees. "Do you really want to know?"

"Of course I do." She swung her legs over to face him, knees touching, she held his hands. "Come on, tell me. We probably have the same thoughts."

He didn't want to tell her his fear, fear that there was someone else they had not considered for the murder, someone who thought if he and Marian were eliminated, they would never be caught. Instead, Charlie decided to talk about the clues they already had.

"We're missing one little piece. I know we are close to solving this thing, but something is nagging in my mind and I can't quite grasp it."

Marian shook her head. "No, I was thinking about dinner and listening to music afterward. Not up for dancing, unless ..." She touched his forehead with hers, "it's real slow dancing," Marian said with a sly grin.

"Oh, I like your thoughts better." Charlie kissed the tip of her nose.

She leaned back. "But I must confess, I did have your same thoughts, too. You don't think Henry and Bella were in on it together, do you?"

"That is a possibility we have to consider. If I only had that missing piece." He looked at his watch. "It's five-forty-five. I'm getting hungry. Where do you want to go?"

Charlie stood and helped Marian up.

"Mm, I don't know. Why don't you call Jack, see if he and Sophia want to join us?"

"I'll do that, but you know, we have to address the fact that we still need to interview Henry and Bella. I'd like to do it before anyone is allowed onshore tomorrow."

"So now, later tonight, or early in the morning?"

"You choose."

Marian smirked. "None sound appealing to me."

"How about this; I'll see if Watson can arrange for both of them to not be allowed off the ship until they meet with us tomorrow after we have breakfast in bed. How does that sound?"

"You are a brilliant man."

Charlie opened the sliding door, stepped into the cabin, and froze.

The bed they had undone when they first returned to the cabin was now made up. There was a plate of chocolate covered strawberries on the dining table and the fruit basket had been replenished.

Charlie looked in the trash cans. Empty. He walked into the bathroom. Fresh towels. The whole cabin had been cleaned and straightened without either one of them hearing someone in their cabin.

"Well, that's kind of creepy," Marian rubbed the goosebumps from her arms. "Us being right outside when Bella and Henry came in without us knowing."

"Yeah." Charlie stood with his fist on his hips. "I know I turned the lock. Huh, I wonder how they got in." He threw up his hands. "Maybe I didn't but in the future, I'll double check, put out the 'Do Not Disturb' sign, and shove a chair under the door knob."

"That should do it. I'm going to get dressed." Marian opened the closet and stared at her clothes. "Do you want to eat at that tapas place or do you want a proper sit-down dinner?"

"Tapas is fine. I'll call Jack and ask if he and Sophia can meet us there. Seven o'clock okay?"

"Perfect," Marian yelled from the bathroom.

Before Charlie made the call, he put out the sign, double checked the lock and put a chair under the door knob. "There! No one should be getting in without a struggle," he mumbled to himself.

The phone rang.

"McClung speaking," Charlie answered in a stern voice. "Hey, Jack! I was just about to call you." His tone lightened. "Yeah, can you and Sophia meet us at the tapas joint around seven o'clock?"

Charlie's grin widened. "Great! Marian wants to find a band to listen to afterward, but no dancing." He nodded. "Yep, see you both there."

♣

Charlie and Marian were the first to arrive at the restaurant. The restaurant was more of a bar, sit where you like. Charlie chose a table strategically placed in the corner, so he could have his back against the wall and see the entrance. Marian sat next to him. They ordered two Coronas and water as they waited for Jack and Sophia.

They entered the nearly empty restaurant and looked around. Charlie stood and waved them over.

"Sophia, you look stunning." Marian admired the red and black matador dress. "What a beautiful shawl. Is it a flamenco dancer's shawl?"

Sophia turned around so Marian could see the rose design on the back. "Yes, I got this outfit when I visited Spain on business a few months back."

Jack ordered beers for him and his sister. "At least this one covers her knees. The one she had on the other night, I swear, it barely covered her butt."

"Stop it, Jack, you sound like our father. How did you ever become such a prude?"

"I married one."

Sophia rolled her eyes. "You and me both. But enough of this dreadful talk. I'm ready to order. Menus?"

Charlie pointed toward a display glass built into the whole length of the bar, filled with a wide variety of appetizers, breads, salads, and desserts. "There's the menu. You walk up there and point to whatever you want."

"Oh, goody!" Sophia clapped her hands. "So glad this dress is stretchy."

"You two go ahead, we'll wait for you to get back. We had a mid-afternoon snack."

Jack and Sophia made their way to the bar.

Marian envied Sophia's model-like figure, tall, long, and lean.

Charlie observed Marian's intense study of Jack's sister as she stood at the bar. "Darling, she's got nothing over you. You're perfection in my eyes."

She blushed. "Is my envy that obvious?"

"I've been around women long enough to know what they're thinking when they see a woman like Sophia." He kissed Marian's cheek. "Venus, Helen of Troy, and Nefertiti would all be envious of your beauty."

Marian began to protest.

Charlie put his index finger on her lips. "Shh, no arguments. I only speak the facts." His attention was pulled away by Sophia's loud squeak of surprise.

Peter stood beside her, laughing. "Sorry about that, didn't mean to spook you." He was alone.

Charlie looked around to see if Bella was lurking in the shadows. She was nowhere in sight.

"I wonder if Peter's appearance is just a happy coincidence." Charlie glanced at Marian. "You know he'll be joining us."

"Yeah, too bad. I wanted to get to know Jack and Sophia better."

An irritated Jack and smiling Sophia returned to the table carrying piled high plates, with Peter trailing behind them, a drink in one hand and a plate in the other.

"Oh, boy, look who found us," Jack said sarcastically as he pulled out the chair closest to Marian for his sister, and then sat next to her, preventing Peter from sitting close to Sophia.

Peter plopped down in the chair closest to Charlie. "Long time no see," he said as he extended his hand to Charlie.

As Charlie shook Peter's limp hand, he could smell the cloud of alcohol surrounding the man. "Hmm, fancy running into you here. I thought you liked a more tantalizing bar."

Peter hunched up his shoulders. "Mmm, variety is the spice of life I say."

Humph, look what that's got him. A dead wife. Charlie wondered if the man ever thought before he spoke. Or if he ever thought about anyone but himself.

"Excuse us while we go get something to eat." Charlie escorted his wife to the bar.

When they returned, Peter was sitting in Marian's seat.

"Peter, if you don't mind, I really would like to sit next to Sophia. You know, girl talk." Marian smiled sweetly, sporting cutie pie eyes.

Peter slid over to the next seat.

"Nope, that's my spot. Back into your original chair." Charlie glared at the drunk man.

Peter obeyed without seeming to notice Charlie's irritation. "I think it's grand that I ran into y'all. My best employee," he tipped his glass toward Sophia, "and my new friends, Jack, Marian, and McClung." He raised his glass for a toast. "To the best pals a man could have."

Charlie raised his glass with the rest of the group. *How sad that we are considered his best pals. We're strangers who happened to be invited to his renewal ceremony simply because we booked a suite. And Jack because he's Sophia's brother. And from Sophia's statements, he's just her boss.*

Peter finished his drink. "Another round, on me. What'll you have? Charlie, another beer?" He snapped his fingers in the air for someone to come to their table. When no one appeared, Peter stood, "I guess I'll go to the bar and get our libations. Give me your order."

"Marian and I are fine for now."

"Me, too," Jack looked at his sister.

"I'll have a Mojito if you're buying." Sophia handed Peter her empty glass. "Be a love and take this with you. The table's a bit crowded."

After Peter was out of hearing range, Charlie looked at Sophia. "Did he know you were going to be here?"

Sophia picked up a date, stuffed with chorizo, wrapped in bacon, and pierced with a toothpick. "No. He must have followed me here. This is the first time I've laid eyes on him all day. Trying to keep my distance until this murder is solved."

She put the date into her mouth, closed her lips and then pulled it off the toothpick, softly moaning as she chewed the savory morsel. Sophia handed Marian one from her plate as she swallowed. "Oh, you've got to try one. It is divine."

"Jack, did he follow you?" Charlie watched Peter flirt with the young woman behind the bar. *The man can't make up his mind if he misses his dead wife or not. Fickle, he is.*

Shrugging, Jack shook his head. "I don't know, sorry."

Peter returned with the Mojito for Sophia in one hand, a bottle of Knappogue Castle 12 single malt Irish whiskey tucked under his arm, and three tumblers hooked between his fingers on his other hand.

Sophia took the Mojito. "They make the best Mojito."

"I had my first one ever today. Two of them," Marian agreed.

Peter sat a tumbler in front of Jack and Charlie, opened the bottle and poured each man two fingers. "McClung, I think you'll enjoy this brand."

"Yes, I've had it before, very smooth. Thank you." Charlie sampled golden liquid and followed it with a sip of water. "Very nice."

"More?" Peter offered the bottle to Charlie.

He waved it away. "One's enough for me, thanks, maybe later."

Peter mellowed with each taste of whisky. He and Sophia shared hilarious sales stories, Charlie entertained them with stupid criminal tales, and Jack with the weirdest autopsy findings. They passed around plates of tapas, then settled on their favorites.

Marian pushed an empty plate away from her. "No more, or I'll explode."

"Ready for some music?" Charlie wrapped his arm around Marian's shoulder.

"Yes, please. Let's go back to the place with the big band."

Sophia jumped up. "Come on, Jack. I'm ready to dance."

"No, McClung said no dancing."

She stamped her foot and pushed out her bottom lip in a pout.

Marian stood and held Charlie's hand. "Let's just decide once we get there. If they don't want to dance, it may be just you and me out on the dance floor, Sophia. Unless it's a slow dance, then you're on your own, girl."

"I think I can handle the slow dancing." Charlie twirled Marian around, clutched her to his chest, and began to sway to the music in his head.

With sad eyes, Peter looked to Charlie. "Do you mind if I tag along? I really don't want to be alone."

Charlie considered his request. *What's that old saying; keep your friends close and your enemies closer? And Peter just may be an enemy.* "Sure, Peter, you can join us."

He grinned like a school boy. "Thanks! Let me have the bar store this whisky for later, that is if y'all don't want anymore. Anyone care for more?" Peter held up the bottle.

"No. We'll wait for you at the entrance." Charlie took a double take toward the bar. He could have sworn he saw Bella duck down behind the display case of tapas.

Chapter 29

"Oh, Charlie, it's the same band," Marian yelled over the music and the noise of the crowded room.

Charlie quickly scanned the room and found a table where the occupants appeared to be on the verge of leaving. He took several long strides, pulling Marian along with him.

"Are you guys about to leave?"

The group looked at Charlie hovering over them and decided to relinquish the table sooner than they had planned.

"Thank you." Charlie pulled out a chair for Marian and then one for Sophia.

Just as they were all seated, the band took a ten-minute break.

"How fortuitous, I can get us some drinks." Peter pointed to Sophia. "Mojito?"

"Sure, why not."

Charlie and Marian asked for Diet Dr Peppers and for Jack, a Corona.

Peter left them alone.

"Marian, do you have a piece of paper and pen in that miniature purse?"

"It's a clutch, and yes I do." Marian opened the small black bag. "Here you go. Going to request your dance music?" Marian teased her husband.

Charlie scribbled on the tiny square. "It's a surprise." He held out the pen. "Anyone else?"

"Give me." Sophia snatched the pen from Charlie's hand. "I think we should all make requests."

They all took turns and waited for Peter to return before giving the scraps of paper to the band leader.

He returned empty handed. "The bar is rather busy. Someone will bring our drinks to us when they're ready."

Sophia shoved the pen into Peter's hand. "Write down a song. We all have. Hurry up before the band starts to play."

She grabbed the paper from Peter, and then shimmied up to the band leader, thrusting the notes at him.

The singer read them and gave them a thumbs up. He then spoke with his band.

"Charlie, I need to go to the restroom before the band starts to play."

He started to stand. Sophia rested her hand on his arm. ""I'll go with her. I need a potty break myself."

The two women hooked arms together, Sophia needed someone to steady her, and then the two women wormed their way to the bathroom.

"Is that some genetic thing; women going in pairs to relieve themselves?" Peter asked Jack.

Jack was bewildered. "How should I know?"

"You're a doctor."

"I'm a medical examiner, not a geneticist. Just because I cut open heads, doesn't mean I can read their minds. Pfft!"

"Oh." Peter looked toward the bar. "I wonder when they'll bring our drinks. I'm getting parched."

Charlie chuckled at Jack's response. He slowly scanned the sea of faces and searched the dark corners while he waited for Marian to return.

The band was on stage preparing to begin their next set.

"Where are those women?" Charlie craned his neck toward the path they had taken to the restroom. "I hope they get back before the band plays my request."

He saw Sophia and the top of Marian's head as they worked their way back to the table. Charlie felt the hair on his neck prickle. Something was wrong. He jumped up and pushed his way to Marian's side.

Marian was pale.

"What happened? What's wrong?" Charlie cradled his wife next to him as he walked toward the table.

"I don't know. Something spooked me on the way back."

"What?"

They sat down, Charlie's arm still around Marian. He brushed her cheek lightly with his fingertips. "Tell me what happened."

"Well, I thought I felt something on my neck … as if someone blew on it. When I turn to see, I thought I heard someone say, bitch, and then I tripped. If it hadn't been for Sophia, I would've fallen flat on my face."

He looked at Sophia.

"I heard it, too."

"Man or woman?"

Both women said, "I don't know."

Marian popped her knuckles. "It was like a loud, throaty whisper, the room was so noisy that I couldn't tell which direction it was coming from. I don't even know if it was meant for me."

Sophia bobbed her head in agreement.

"Did someone trip you on purpose?"

Marian bit her lips and shook her head. "I don't know. It could have been a chair. So many people, I can't say for sure."

"You stay here. I'm going to look around over there."

"Why? If someone said it to me and if they tripped me on purpose, they're probably long gone." Marian held onto his hand.

Charlie hated seeing that look in her eyes, anxiety and confusion. He ran his fingers through her hair. "I should have gone with you." Charlie wrapped his arms around her. "I'm sorry, so sorry."

"I'll go take a look around, stay with them." Jack stood. "Come with me, Peter." The two men retraced the women's path.

"It's not your fault. I'm probably making a big deal out of nothing." Marian leaned away and held onto his shoulders as she looked into his eyes. "I'm fine, really." She glanced down at the table. "Where are the drinks? I really need something to drink; my mouth feels like cotton."

Jack and Peter sat down. "She's right. There's really nothing to find, just a bunch of people milling around."

Charlie held on to Marian's forearms and looked squarely into her eyes. "Are you sure you're okay, any scrapes or cuts that Doctor Nelson should look at?"

Marian looked at her knees and elbows. "Maybe some bruises but that's all. Really, I'm fine, honest."

"Okay, you sit here, I need to satisfy my curiosity." Charlie looked at Jack. "Keep an eye on her."

He nodded. "We all will, won't we?" Jack looked around the table, everyone agreed to protect Marian.

Satisfied, Charlie went to the end of the bar closest to the restrooms. "Hey, did you see the lady who fell a few minutes ago?"

The bartender's eyes bugged out. "No! Is she okay? Do I need to call the medical team?"

"No need to do that, she's fine but someone tripped her. Just trying to find out what piece of crap would do that to a lady."

"I'm sorry, mate, I wish I could help you."

"Yeah, me, too. Sorry to bother you."

"Can I get you anything to drink?"

Charlie shook his head. "No, we placed an order a while ago, still waiting for them to arrive at our table." He pointed toward their spot.

"I'll make sure you get your drinks, ASAP." The bartender turned away to check on their order.

Charlie pushed away from the edge of the bar. Something white lying on bar caught his eye. Bits of a torn napkin forming a heart, just like the one he found earlier in the day.

"Hey!" Charlie called the bartender back.

"Need something else?"

"Tell me, who was sitting here, right here?" Charlie stabbed the center of the heart with his index finger, his heart pounded with the frantic need to know who was toying with them.

The bartender's face fell, he licked his lips like a scared cat. "Sorry, again, mate, I don't remember. The place's been packed all night, people coming and going." He shook his head. "Sorry, I really wish I could remember."

Charlie grimaced, "It's all right, I understand. Thanks, anyway." He searched the sea of faces, hoping to catch a glimpse of someone watching him or Marian. No one looked the least bit suspicious. With an anger-filled swipe, he scattered the pieces like withered fall leaves on a blustery day.

He stood clenching and unclenching his fists, taking deep breaths to calm his fury. After a few seconds, he had taken control of his emotions. Charlie walked back calmly to Marian, not wanting to cause her to worry. He smiled as he sat down and her countenance relaxed with his grin.

"The bartender didn't see anything but he is checking on our drink order."

The band began to play.

"Do you know that song?" Charlie leered at Marian.

She grinned shyly. "Uhuh."

Charlie offered his hand to her as he stood. "Shall we?"

"Let's."

She clasped his open hand, he pulled her close, and they swayed slowly out onto the vacant dance floor.

Charlie wanted her to forget about the dark shadows and think of their bright future together. He brushed his lips against her ear and softly sang with the band, "I've been waiting for a girl like you to come into my life."

"Mm, you know how to make a girl quiver. Is this your song?"

"But of course." Charlie wanted to relax, enjoy this small moment of bliss but his mind was focused on keeping Marian safe. Every corner looked sinister, every sudden moment was a threat, but he was thankful for her resiliency.

He had witnessed her blossom in their three months together, from quiet and forlorn, to lively and cheerful. She had found a framed cross-stitched quote and hung it over the alarm panel, *Worry is like a rocking chair. It gives you something to do, but it doesn't get you anywhere,* words to live by she said.

Marian rubbed his back. "Relax, sweetie, everything is all right."

Her warm breath on his neck sidetracked Charlie's thoughts to more pleasant ones. He closed his eyes, enjoyed the scent of her perfume and the feel of her body pressed close to his. Charlie kissed her temple and then opened his eyes. His eyes bugged when he saw the waitress delivering drinks to their table. Bella!

"What the …" Charlie jerked up his head.

"What's wrong?"

Charlie heard the panic in Marian's voice and he felt like punching himself in the head. "Nothing. I'm shocked that Bella is our waitress."

Marian looked around him. "You're kidding." She looked up at her husband. "She's stalking Peter."

"Yep, looks like." Charlie decided, at the moment, Bella could wait, Marian was more important. "Let's finish our dance. We're in the middle of the ocean; she's not going anywhere."

Marian smiled and snuggled deeper into Charlie's arms.

When the song ended, Charlie walked slowly back to the table, not wanting to delve into the reason why Bella was, once again, waiting tables. *Doesn't the girl ever rest?*

Charlie lightly punched Peter's shoulder as he passed by him. "I see your favorite waitress is back."

"I didn't tell her where I was going to be. I can promise you that." Peter didn't look at all thrilled to see his groupie.

"You know, I think I saw her at the tapas joint when we left." Charlie grinned. "I think she's your number one fan."

"I'm afraid of her, especially after last night." Peter finished his drink. "Crap!" He flicked his finger against the empty glass. "Now she'll be over here. Again."

Sophia leaned forward from between Jack and Marian. "What happened last night?"

"Probably performance problems," Jack snorted.

"No," Peter growled. "She attacked me, and not in a good way."

Sophia's mouth dropped open. "Attacked you! Why?"

"Sins of my youth."

Jack blurted, "She's your daughter!"

"Let him explain, I'd like to hear it again." Charlie leaned back, held his Diet Dr Pepper and then motioned for Peter to begin. "Regale us with the tale of how your past sins have come to haunt you."

Peter glared at them.

"Better hurry, here she comes," Marian mumbled behind her glass.

He leaned forward and whispered loudly, "Years ago, I went out with her mother and I was stupid enough to have my picture taken with her. I have no clue how she got hold of the picture. Bella confronted me last night with the picture. Accusing me of all sorts of things that I don't care to go into. Embarrassing."

"Shhh, she's almost here," Marian warned.

Bella set down a fresh drink in front of Peter. "Here you go. I noticed your glass was empty." She smiled sweetly. "Can I get anyone anything?"

Peter sat stiffly with a sick look on his face while everyone else grinned and said no.

"All right then, I'll be right over there if you need me." Bella addressed her reply toward Peter.

He nodded, barely.

Charlie watched her go to the spot she had indicated. He felt his drink catch in his throat, quickly swallowed, and then coughed.

Marian patted him on his back. "Are you okay?"

"Yeah," he coughed again, "Henry. It's Henry next to her."

The group turned and looked.

"I'm beginning to think there's more to their relationship than either one of them is letting on." Charlie wiped his mouth and nose with one of the cocktail napkins strewn on the table. "I think I'll go have a word with him."

Marian placed her hand lightly on his shoulder as he began to stand. "Let's keep tonight to just us. Like you said, we're in the middle of the ocean. Where is Henry going to go? Hmm?"

He looked at her serene face and relaxed. "You're right."

The band began to play, "Night and Day".

Sophia grabbed her brother's arm, jerking him up with her. "Come on, Jacky Boy, that's my song. You remember?"

Jack groaned, "Why, oh, why did our mother send me to Arthur Murray's Dance Studio? What evil did I do to deserve such punishment?"

Sophia laughed and kissed his cheek. "Oh, you love it! You can pretend to hate it all you want, but you know you love it."

He shrugged his shoulders and grinned. "Let's strut."

Charlie watched Jack and Sophia twirl and dip, amazed at how graceful Jack was. The brother-sister team put on quite a show; the other dancers stood back, amazed by their skill. But Charlie split his gaze between the dance floor and the pair by the bar, Henry and Bella.

Henry was speaking into Bella's ear, her constant smile waned to a frown and then back to a grin. She said something to him and whatever she said made Henry look right at Charlie. Henry's countenance was like stone. He turned and walked out of the bar.

Charlie wanted to follow Henry, ask him what was going on between him and Bella, and what Peter meant to the both of them. He wanted to crack open both of their heads, to read their thoughts, to find out what secrets and lies were buried in the dark recesses.

His attention was drawn back to the dance floor when he heard clapping. Charlie clapped and stood to welcome the dance stars back to their seats. He glanced back towards Bella but she was nowhere in sight.

Charlie patted Marian's hand. "Gotta run to the restroom right quick. Do you want me to get you anything from the bar?"

"Since you offered, another Pepper."

He leaned over and kissed her cheek. "As you wish."

Charlie caught up with Bella as she stepped outside the bar.

"Bella, hold up just a minute, I have a question for you."

She turned with the ever-present smile on her face. "Ask away."

"Was your mother still married when Peter dated her?"

Bella looked surprised; this was not a question she had expected. "No, my father was dead. Died a few months before she met Peter."

"What about Henry's? Was his mother married when Peter went out with her?"

Bella's mouth popped open. "How did you know about that?"

"I'm a damn good detective."

"Yes, she was. Henry's father found out and abandoned both of them."

Charlie nodded. "Thanks, that's all." He turned and left Bella standing there.

Chapter 30

"Stop following him!" Henry was nose to nose with Bella.

She pushed him away. "You're not my father."

"No, I am not but somebody has to keep you in line. You are going to get yourself in trouble. Stay away from Mr. Ferguson. He is nothing but trouble."

"His name is Peter." Bella began to pace in the small supply room. "I think he owes me."

Henry's eyes bulged. "Owes you! Owes you what?"

"I don't know," the young woman whined as she searched for a box of frilly toothpicks. "But he should pay."

"Look what has happened to the women in his life. They are ruined or die! Stay away from him."

"Pssh, like anything like that will happen to me. I've got brains, plans, and schemes. I can take care of myself. Nothing's happened to me so far and it won't!"

"At the rate you are going, you are going to end up in serious trouble."

Bella found the toothpicks. She turned, holding the box protectively against her chest. Bella studied Henry, and wished she could read his mind, wished she could figure him out. He kept his desires, dreams, and demons locked up inside. Bella thought about telling him about McClung's questions about their parents but she didn't want to upset him anymore than he was already. She loved him, but only as a brother and Henry cared deeply for her, but in what way, she wasn't sure. All she knew was that any crime she could ever commit, he would stand by her side. Protect her. But right now, he was getting in her way.

"Oh, Henry, lighten up. He'll be gone in four days." She grinned wickedly.

Henry's jaw muscles flexed as he clinched his teeth. "Why do you insist on being so obstinate?"

Bella laughed. "Me? I think you're the one being pig-headed." She circled around him, her fingers brushed lightly against him as if she were winding a rope around him. "Just let me have some fun. I promise not to get caught."

"I don't want to see you get hurt."

Bella stopped in front of Henry, put her arms around his neck, laced her fingers together, and pulled his head close to hers. She licked her lips and then softly brushed them across his. "I can't get hurt. Remember? I have a heart that's blacker and sharper than obsidian glass."

Chapter 31

Charlie opened their cabin door and ushered Marian quickly inside.

"Mmm, this was a great night; good food, good friends, good music, and dancing," she sighed.

I'm glad she's dismissed the tripping incident. Charlie knew who killed Tammy but decided to delay that thought until tomorrow. He didn't want anything to spoil what was left of this night. Once inside the cabin, he pulled her around into his arms and kissed her, letting her know that the best was yet to come.

They made it to the king-size bed, leaving a trail of clothes in their wake. Charlie cradled her in his arms as they fell onto the bed, pillows tossed on the floor, bedcoverings flung to the side.

A loud bang and the sound of angry voices disturbed them, instantly breaking the mood.

"What the ..." Charlie rolled over into a sitting position. "Do you hear that?"

Marian sat beside her husband. "Yeah, sounds like it's coming from the Ferguson suite. I wonder if Peter is okay. He said he wasn't feeling well."

Charlie went to look out the peephole. He could see light shining on the wall opposite the Ferguson's suite which could only mean the door was open. At this time of night, it should be closed. He felt dread climbing up his spine. "Call Watson and Doctor Nelson, their cards are under the phone. Tell them to get here now!"

He grabbed his pants from the floor, quickly put them on, and was out the door. Standing with his ear to the open door, Charlie wished for his gun as he listened.

Sounds of groaning drifted from the brightly-lit cabin and he could hear a struggle out on the balcony. Charlie kicked open the door. The doorknob hit the wall with such force that it stuck in the sheetrock. He cleared the bathroom before entering the bedroom.

Bella lay on the floor beside the dresser, a deep gash on her forehead, blood oozed from the open wound. Blood was on the dresser's edge. Her long braid was no longer wrapped around her head but around her neck. Charlie heard her groan and knew she was alive.

He moved quickly toward the balcony, kicking furniture out of his way. The chairs and table on the balcony made horrible screeching noises. Lights from the balcony next door cast an eerie glow, revealing three bodies bouncing off the furniture. Charlie heard the sounds of fists hitting flesh and men cursing. He turned on the balcony lights.

Henry had Peter in a choke hold, trying to push him over the high balcony rails into the ocean. Antonio was beating Henry on his back, shoulders, and head, struggling to prevent him from flipping Peter overboard.

Charlie pulled Antonio to the side, grabbed a handful of Henry's hair, yanking it as hard as he could. Henry's head jerked backward. He released his grip from Peter's neck. Peter collapsed to the floor, gasping for breath as he held his neck protectively.

Henry turned and took a swing at Charlie.

Charlie deflected the punch and landed his own on Henry's jaw. The blow increased Henry's fury. He back-peddled a few steps and stood heaving, casting drops of spit into the air.

The guy's insane. Charlie jumped aside as Henry lunged violently toward him.

"Antonio! Get Peter inside," Charlie yelled.

Henry went after Antonio.

Charlie enveloped Henry in a bear-hug before he could reach Antonio.

Henry slammed himself backward against the wall.

The wind rushed from Charlie's lungs. He gasped for breath and hung on for dear life, pushed away from the wall, and rammed Henry against the railing.

Henry hung onto the rail, flinging his body side-to-side, like a dog shaking water from his fur, as he tried to rid himself of Charlie.

Charlie released Henry and gave him a sucker punch to his kidneys.

Henry spun around; he swung wildly past Charlie's nose and then surprised him with a punch to the temple.

Charlie staggered back as Henry propelled forward, but he was ready for him and landed a good uppercut to Henry's chin. He thought Henry was going to go down. Instead, Henry stood staring at him, shook it off and then assumed a boxer's stance.

"All right then, let's finish this," Charlie landed a punch on Henry's nose, followed by a left hook to his jaw, and then a crushing blow to his gut.

Henry roared in pain as he flailed blindly at Charlie.

Charlie blocked most of the blows and the fight continued, his fists making solid contact to Henry's body.

Marian ran out onto the balcony, horrified as she witnessed Henry and Charlie pummeling each other. She glanced around the small space for a weapon of some sort. Miraculously, a bottle of Aberfeldy had survived the melee and was lying on top of the table. She quickly grabbed it, bashed it against Henry's head, causing him to collapse to the floor.

Charlie leaned back on the wall; his chest was heaving, blood beaded on his lip and under his nose.

Marian gave Henry a swift kick to his stomach. "That's for hurting my Charlie." And then she stepped on him as she made her way to her husband.

Charlie wiped away the blood on his face and laughed, "Remind me never to get in a fight with you. You fight dirty."

"I'm a girl. I've got to do what I have to." She hugged him gently. "Oh, Charlie, are you hurt bad?"

"No, baby, I'm fine, just fine."

Officer Watson ran out onto the balcony. "What the bloody hell happened?"

"I caught our murderer." Charlie massaged his jaws with one hand, his other hand was rubbing Marian's head, comforting not only her but himself as well. "There he is." He nodded toward Henry lying at his feet.

Watson looked down. "Henry?"

"Yep, Henry."

"Come over here," Watson instructed the security guard standing in the balcony doorway. "Cuff him and lock him up."

Henry groaned as the guard clamped the cold, biting metal around his wrists.

"Have the doctor look at the cut on his head before you take him away." Watson looked at Charlie. "What about you? You should have Nelson look at you."

Marian stepped back and ran her fingers over his face. "Yes, Charlie, please, just to be on the safe side." She took his hands and examined his knuckles and gently kissed them. "Oh, what a fine mess."

Doctor Nelson walked out onto the balcony. "Holy cow! More out here?"

"Is Bella going to be okay?" Charlie slid his arm across Marian's shoulders, pushed away from the wall, stepped over Henry, and headed inside.

"Nasty cut and a concussion. She'll need stitches." The doctor squatted down to examine Henry's bloody head. "Hmm, appears to be superficial, nothing serious." His gloved fingers probed Henry's bloody head. "I'd say a concussion, too, but I'll know more once we get him in the examining room. The thing about head wounds, even minor ones, is they bleed like crazy."

Doctor Nelson stood, removed his bloody gloves and followed Charlie and Marian inside. "Sit down and let me take a look at you."

Charlie picked up a chair and sat down. Marian stood behind him, rubbing his shoulders.

The doctor removed an ophthalmoscope from his well-used, black leather medical bag. "Eyes look okay." He lightly touched each bruise and cut on Charlie's face. "No stitches needed, just a bit of cleaning up."

"So, I'm going to live, doc?"

"A bit beat up, but, yep, you're gonna live." Doctor Nelson removed a few cotton wipes from his bag, moistened them with antiseptic, and began to clean Charlie's cuts and scrapes, beginning with his face. "You're going to have some swelling and a few colorful bruises."

The doctor chuckled. "Not gonna be a pretty boy for a week or three."

Marian kissed the top of her husband's head. "You will always be the most handsome man in the universe to me."

Peter stumbled over to Charlie's side. "Thank you for saving my life."

"Antonio's the one you should be thanking; I only assisted." Charlie looked around the room. "Where is he, anyway?"

Doctor Nelson answered, "He's sitting out in the hallway."

Peter weaved his way toward the open door.

"Are we finished doc?" Charlie stood to follow Peter.

The doctor nodded and motioned for him to go.

Charlie found Peter sitting next to Antonio, neither one speaking.

"Antonio, how did you know Henry killed Tammy?"

"Didn't really. I figured it had to be either Bella or Henry. After Shannon told me Bella was with Peter that night, I knew it must have been Henry. All I wanted was to hear it from his lips. I wanted him to tell me why, why he killed the only woman I ever really loved."

Peter cleared his throat. "Thank you for saving my life. It must've been hard."

"Why?" Antonio looked puzzled.

"Well, because … because you loved Tammy and I treated her so badly."

Antonio swallowed hard. Tears ran down his cheeks. "Yes, I did love her and I hated the way you treated her, but I never wanted you dead."

Peter hesitantly put his arm over Antonio's shoulders as they both cried softly over the death of Tammy whom they both loved, differently.

Chapter 32

Charlie spent the morning with Marian. They slept late and had breakfast in their suite. Marian waited on him, hand and foot. She smoothed the ointment Doctor Nelson had given her over his wounds as he soaked in a hot bath with Epsom salts.

"Some honeymoon, huh?" Charlie held her hand and kissed her palm.

"No one can claim their honeymoon was more exciting than ours. Besides, it all turned out well." She lightly patted his bruised hand. "We still have each other, scraped, bruised and battered, but all in one piece."

He sighed. "I'll be glad when it's completely over, not our honeymoon," Charlie quickly corrected, "the investigation."

"It'll be over today and we have three days left. Thank goodness we booked a ten-day cruise." Marian ran her hand over Charlie's close-cropped hair.

"Five more minutes in the tub and we'll go wrap up the investigation."

Marian shook her head. "I think I'll pass. I just want to sit on our balcony and read. You can fill me in when it's over and done with."

Charlie squeezed her knee as she sat on the side of the tub. He understood and was glad she wanted no part of the final questioning.

He had one nagging question, nothing to do with Tammy's murder but with Marian.

Marian hadn't mentioned it and he wasn't going to bring it up, but he couldn't figure out who was following Marian. After last night's incident, he knew it was Marian they were following and not him. But why? And was it Bella or Henry or some complete stranger? Would he ever know? He hoped it was just some random idiot thinking it was all a joke. A cruel and sick joke that is, and once off the ship, Marian would never encounter them again.

♣

Charlie and Officer Watson questioned Bella, Peter, and Antonio first, saving Henry for last. Not much was learned from them. Peter was drunk and oblivious to anyone around him, left the door unlocked, and Bella followed him into the cabin.

Bella tried to seduce him but before she could, Henry came in. He jerked her braid, wrapped it around her neck, and then slung her away from Peter. When Bella hit her head on the dresser, Henry became enraged, blaming Peter for making him do that to her.

Antonio came in when he heard Henry yelling. He found Henry with his arms around Peter, dragging him out onto the balcony. If Antonio had not been following Henry, Peter would be at the bottom of the ocean.

Charlie learned from Bella that Peter was just a game to her. She wanted to toy with him just like he did with her mother. Her mother was angry at him, hated him even, never trusted another man, but she eventually moved on, unlike Henry's mother.

Bella said that her plan was to marry Peter, take everything she could from him, and then leave him penniless, in the same way he left her mother with nothing but empty promises. Well, except for the stupid picture.

After Peter left without even a goodbye, Bella said her mother and grandmother became overprotective and stifling, never allowing her any friends, much less a boyfriend, saying they didn't want her to get hurt. They only trusted Henry.

She giggled, "If they only knew how I toyed with him." Throwing her head back in defiance, Bella confessed, "Well, thanks to them I learned to never fall in love, just take what I can get and move on." She grinned. "Boy, I would've loved to have been able to waltz into my grandmother's house with Peter by my side and say, look at me. I've got what you wanted and couldn't get."

"I don't understand why you would want to hurt your mother and grandmother like that." Charlie was confused by Bella's need to punish them.

"My mother was weak and needy; letting some man get the best of her. And my grandmother, coddling her like she was a child. My father taught me to use my backbone, never depend on some man to make me happy." Bella stared at Charlie. "My father said I had brains and beauty and for me to use them to the best of my ability." Her nose flared with the pride she was feeling.

"But why would your father tell you something like that? Weren't you just a little girl?" Charlie still couldn't see through Bella's muddled explanation.

"My father knew he was dying. He didn't want me to be like them, depending on someone who may not be around. He wanted me to be my own person, to be able to stand on my own two legs for support."

Bella huffed, "They told me real ladies need a man to love them, protect them, and care for them. But look what that got them! Nothing! I wanted more. My father wanted more for me. But they … they wanted me to be just like them, lonely and broken." She violently rubbed away the tears running down her cheeks. "God, what century are they living in?"

"May I go now? I've answered all of your questions." Bella stood to leave. "Are you charging me with anything?"

Charlie arched his left eyebrow, still not understanding Bella's warped thought process but he was tired of pursuing what appeared to him just a vast vortex of confused reasoning. "No, you haven't broken any laws; I don't know about the ship's rule. But I have one more question, Bella. Were you following Marian?"

Bella shook her head. "No, why would I do a thing like that?"

"No reason, just asking. You may leave now, that is if Officer Watson has no further questions."

Watson spoke firmly. "Bella, when you finish your duties, I want you in my office today. Do you understand that?'

"Yes, sir." Bella waited for him to dismiss her.

Officer Watson waved her away.

♣

Charlie and Officer Watson went into the holding cell to question him. Two guards with weapons stood just outside the door.

Charlie took the lead.

A table with three chairs had been placed in the small room. Charlie set down a small box of evidence and a tape recorder, turned it on and then read Henry his rights.

"Henry, do you understand your rights?

He nodded.

"You need to answer the question aloud."

"Yes," Henry answered in a voice just above a whisper.

"Henry, how are you feeling this morning?"

He shrugged and stared at his pale, bruised hands lying limply on his lap.

"Would you like something to drink, Henry?"

Henry turned his head and stared at a spot on the floor. He shook his head and said, "No."

"Okay, no water." Charlie opened the box and removed a small glass jar with tiny brownish-black specks inside, some lay still in the bottom of the container, while others bounced around. He held it up for Henry to see.

"Henry, are these fleas?"

"Yes."

"Please explain why we found a jar of fleas in your cabin."

Henry sneered, "Those were for Peter. I never got a chance to use them." He stared past Charlie. "I was standing just outside of Peter's cabin the morning after his wife died. I was staring at the peephole, thinking how I was in control of his destiny, and the word fleas just popped into my head." He bit his finger to keep himself from laughing.

"Why fleas?"

"A bit of irritation, torture for Peter. Just a tiny taste of the suffering he has been responsible for."

Charlie removed another piece of evidence from the box and set it on the table, a small, glass petri dish containing two stingers with venom sacs. Next, he placed a thin syringe, a bottle of peanut oil, and a bottle of DMSO beside the petri dish. The last thing he removed was a worn, black diary.

"Henry, did you kill Tammy?"

He looked at all of the evidence staring him in the face. "Yes," he sighed.

Charlie looked at Watson, both relieved.

"All right. Can you tell me why, Henry, why did you kill Tammy?"

He sat very still, only his nostrils flared as his chest expanded with each breath. Licking his dry lips, he looked up, his eyes shifted between Charlie and Officer Watson. "I think I'd like some water, now."

Officer Watson motioned to one of the guards to get water for Henry. They waited until the man returned.

Henry drank all of the water in the small paper cup. "Thank you."

"Would you like some more water?"

"No."

"Okay, let's begin. Henry, why did you kill Tammy?"

Henry's lips trembled. "I did it for my mama and grandmother."

Charlie glanced at Watson who shook his head.

"What did Tammy do to your mama and grandmother to deserve to die the way she did? It was a horrible death. You know that, don't you?"

He looked directly at Charlie. "My mama suffered for months until she couldn't take it anymore and killed herself." Henry's voice was hard, anger flamed in his cheeks. "I was left alone with my grandmother. She drilled it into my head, day in and day out, that Peter Ferguson was nothing but filth who didn't deserve anyone, anyone to love him."

"I don't understand why your mama killed herself."

Henry gritted his teeth. "Mama loved him, threw everything away because of his promises. Daddy left me, left us. I never saw my daddy again because of him. We were forced to live with my grandmother."

Charlie let Henry seethe for a few moments before he asked the next question.

"I'm sorry Henry, I still don't understand why she killed herself."

He pointed his chin toward the diary. "You have that, those are her words. You know why," Henry spat bitterly.

"I want to hear it in your own words," Charlie said as soothingly as possible.

Henry's chest began to heave. "They called her puta! All my so-called friends called my mama a puta. A WHORE!" His head rolled back as he sobbed. "My mama was beautiful, so full of life." He snapped his head forward, "But then, he came along. Beguiled her, used her, filled her full of empty promises and then he tossed her away like a piece of rotten meat. Mama prayed that his wife would die."

A look of disbelief was on his face. "I couldn't believe my sweet, sweet mama wanted someone to die just so that miserable, putrid excuse of a human being would return and make her his wife."

Henry scratched his head and then ran the back of his hand under his nose, wiping away a drip. "But when a few months passed by and he didn't return, mama stopped eating, caring about herself, stopped caring about everything." He paused.

Tears streamed down his cheeks, and he whispered, "Me. She forgot about me." Henry inhaled deeply and then continued. "She was just an empty shell of herself. Peter had sucked the life from my mama. She just wasted away, drowned her pain and misery in alcohol. And then one day, I found her lying on the bed all still and quiet, an empty bottle of pills by her side and a note that simply said, *I'm sorry for being such a fool.*"

He grimaced. "All because of him! He ruined her and our family. My saintly grandmother became a bitter, mean old woman. And my mama, a corpse!" Henry slammed his fist on the table. "Peter Ferguson destroyed everything I loved." He looked longingly at the diary. His fingers stretched toward it then recoiled.

Charlie and Watson sat quietly, waited for Henry's breathing to return to normal.

"Would you like more water?" Not waiting for a response from Henry, Officer Watson looked at the youngest guard, "Get us all some water."

"Henry, I have a few more questions." Charlie leaned forward, resting his forearms on the table. "Why did you take a job on a cruise ship and why this particular company?"

Henry snorted. "He used to tell mama about his favorite cruise line, the best he said, went every year he said, and he told her how she would love it, too." He clicked his tongue. "Mama took his words as a promise that one day he would take her on a cruise. She'd talk about all the exotic places they'd go and the beautiful clothes she'd wear on the ship. And how she'd be treated like a queen on board."

His shoulders sagged as if the depressing memories weighed him down.

The guard returned with a bucket of iced bottled water.

Henry took one, held the unopened bottle between his hands. He sucked his teeth and continued. "After mama died, grandmother could speak of nothing but how the man should be punished, tortured, everything he loved destroyed. She cursed him every day."

He opened the bottle, took a sip, and continued, "So I decided to be on that ship one day and take my revenge. I waited a long time. I was beginning to think that day would never come. Then, poof, here he was with his wife, and of all things, celebrating thirty-five years of wedded bliss."

Henry looked at Charlie and Officer Watson. "She wasn't happy. You both know that. Their marriage was a sham."

"You say that as a fact. Why?" Charlie opened a bottle of water and sipped.

"Are you serious?" Henry snorted, "I followed Peter. I saw how he flirted with any woman who showed him any hint of interest. He totally ignored his wife. The only time the two of them were together was at meal times, even then, they barely spoke to one another."

Henry drained his bottle of water and crunched it into a small cube. "She had to die to pay for his sins. For all the pain and agony he caused."

"But how did you know she was allergic to bees?" Charlie found it interesting that Henry never gave up waiting for his day of revenge and was impressed and how well thought out his plan was.

"One day a bee got into the house. Mama started to laugh and said 'if only his wife would get stung'. I asked her why. She laughed harder and said, 'she'll die, my sweet Henry, one little bee can make my dreams come true'." I didn't understand what she meant at first, but later I realized that Peter must have told Mama that Tammy was allergic to bee stings. It was just too perfect.

"And the peanut oil, how did you know about that?"

Henry snickered, "Mama said Peter loved peanut butter sandwiches. Mama thought it was strange that a rich man who could afford to eat steak and lobster every night only wanted a poor man's sandwich. Every time he came into the restaurant, she'd fix him one. When he'd finish eating it, he'd say, 'I can't get that at home; the wifey's allergic.' Then he'd laugh about how terrified she was of a single little nut."

He looked at Charlie and Officer Watson and said, "He's a filthy pig. I can only imagine how he laughed at my mama, so easily manipulated by him." Henry then crossed his arms, a scowl darkened his face, and he stared at the bottle of peanut oil.

Officer Watson asked, "How did you recognize Peter Ferguson?"

"Are you kidding me?" Henry snorted, "Mama had pictures of him everywhere in her room, practically a shrine. And grandmother used his name in vain every single day."

Officer Watson smirked and nodded.

Charlie asked, "Okay, I want to know how you did it. What did you do that day?"

Inhaling deeply, Henry exhaled hard and then began. "My plan was to kill his wife by making it look like an allergic reaction. I had peanut oil and DMSO, easy enough to keep on board without anyone being suspicious but I couldn't keep live bees on board, that would draw too much attention. Years ago, I met a man on the islands who keeps bees. He's a friend of mine and I knew if I asked him for a few stingers, he would give them to me, no questions asked. When I saw Peter board the ship, I knew it was time to get what I needed."

Henry smirked, "I should've gotten away with it too; what are the odds that a detective and a medical examiner would both be on this cruise? I couldn't plan for that."

It dawned on Charlie that Henry was now using contractions when he spoke. *Strange*.

"That's when you saw me at port. After I met my friend, I saw Peter with Bella and followed them. I had to be there if she needed me.

All she wanted from Peter was to seduce him and get all she could out of him. Maybe become his mistress or even his wife. But for some reason, he didn't seem to be that interested in her. I didn't want Bella to end up like my mama or her mother as far as that goes. But I digress."

Henry grabbed another bottle of water, opened it, and then took a long drink. "I noticed that Tammy brushed her teeth each night before going to bed."

He took another drink. "I can see, Detective McClung you're curious how I know that."

Charlie shrugged.

"I watch my guests. I study them. I notice everything about them. That's what makes me an outstanding butler." Henry grinned. "Anyway, I waited for a time when I knew Peter would be out of the cabin for a while and she would be alone. But I needed an excuse to be in the cabin at the same time when she would be there all by herself."

He paused with a euphoric smile. "Bingo! That night she called and requested towels and wine. I saw Peter in the bar being entertained by Bella, just a happy coincidence, and that meant Tammy was alone, so I set my plan in motion. I rubbed her toothbrush with the peanut oil laced with DMSO." He pointed toward the syringe. "I used that to inject the toothpaste with the oil."

Charlie held up his hand. "And you knew it was her toothbrush because it was pink."

"Yes, of course. May I continue?" Henry appeared to be annoyed by Charlie's interruption.

"Please."

"After I rubbed the handle with the oil, I carefully put the stingers in the brush. She thought I was tidying up the bathroom."

Henry bit his lips. "For a second, I felt a tiny twinge of sadness because I had to kill her but when I walked out of the bathroom, she told me to pick up a wadded up mint wrapper and toss it in the trash can. Really? She couldn't do that herself." He shook his head. "I was beginning to see another side of her. Then she ordered me to pour the trail mix in a bowl. Again, she couldn't do that?"

Henry tapped the water bottle on the table. "She asked me to open the wine. I had no problem with that, but the thing I couldn't figure out was why she wanted two wine glasses set out. I knew Peter was partying it up with Bella, so I had to ask her. She barked at me like I was her lowly servant. But now … now I know who the second glass was for, Antonio."

Henry shook his head, "Who would've thought? Anyway, I got worried because she had to brush her teeth and be alone so no one could help her. I couldn't have someone come in and rescue her. She had to die. Had to die that night. But fortunately for me, not so for her, it was Antonio and he was tending bar until midnight." Henry paused as he finished his water.

He continued. "I waited outside of her cabin, listening for sounds of her dying. When I heard her gasping and banging around in the cabin, I went in and watched her die, like I watched my mama, but Tammy only suffered for a few minutes, not months like my mama did. But it was still satisfying."

Henry smirked, "She looked at me and even with the bulging eyes and balloon-like head; I could see the confusion cloud her face. I saw her struggle to beg me to help her."

He slowly shook his head. "I explained to her that Peter had killed my mama and that she had to be sacrificed to atone for her husband's evil deed. When she stopped struggling, I gave her a good kick just to make sure she was dead." He chuckled, "Dead as dirt."

Henry sat back, crossed his arms, and wore a satisfied smile on his face.

"Henry, I must say, this is one of the most bizarre, well-thought out, and patient murders I have ever run across." Charlie tugged his earlobe. "Yep, most bizarre."

"Thank you. It's very satisfying to see a dream come to fruition. But I think it could have been even better if I had only been able to dump Peter into the sea."

Henry scratched his neck. "Yeah, if only Bella hadn't gotten in the way. I didn't mean to hurt her you know. Peter caused that. You do realize that, don't you?"

Officer Watson stood. "I think I've heard enough."

"This interview has officially ended." Charlie turned off the recorder and walked out with Officer Watson.

But before he exited the room, Charlie stopped and stared at Henry.

"Have you been following Marian?"

Henry pulled his head back in shock. "No! Why would I do something like that? She's a lovely lady."

Chapter 33

Charlie rang his cabin to tell Marian he was coming. He didn't want to startle her by just walking in on her. The phone rang ten times and then rolled into voicemail. He felt panic clutching at his gut. *No, don't get worried, she's probably asleep on the balcony and didn't hear the phone.*

He raced up the twelve flights of stairs and ran to his cabin. A single, tiny piece of white paper was in front of their door. *Oh, God, please no.* He flung open the door. The cabin was empty. Charlie jogged to the balcony. He saw her lying on the chaise, floppy hat covering her face, her slender hand dangling over the edge, a hardback on the floor. Diet Dr Pepper puddled underneath the lounger from the glass lying on its side.

Oh, God, no. No, no, no. In two long strides, he was kneeling by her side. "Marian, are you okay, honey? Marian!" He jiggled her hand.

With a sudden, deep gasp, she sat up. "What, what?" Her hand pressed her chest just over her heart. "Charlie! You scared me!"

Thank you, God. Thank you. He pulled her into his arms. "I'm sorry. It's been a rough morning."

"It's over, right? The Ferguson business is over. Please tell me it's over."

"Yeah, it's finished," He whispered into her ear. "It's just you and me, baby, for three whole days." Charlie stood up, pulled over the other chaise and sat across from his wife. "Tell me what you want to do. We'll do anything you want, just name it."

Marian swung her legs over the edge of the chaise planting her feet in between Charlie's. She grinned. "Anything?"

He liked the wicked look in her eyes and nodded.

She stood and held out her hand. "Come with me. I think we should lay down and consider our options."

"As you wish."

Marian led him inside the cabin and pulled the curtains closed.

— The End —

About The Author

I am the author of The Charlie McClung mysteries, including *Brilliant Disguise and A Good Girl.* I live in Georgia with my husband of 34+ years and a new addition to our household, a Tuxedo cat named Gertrude.

Thank you for taking the time to read *Criminal Kind.* If you enjoyed it, please consider telling your friends and posting a short review on Amazon and Goodreads. Word of mouth is an author's best friend and is very much appreciated.

The fourth book in the series, *Sins of My Youth,* will be released in the winter of 2015.

You can find me on Facebook, Pinterest, LinkedIn, Goodreads, Google+, and Twitter. I invite you to visit my website,

http://maryanneedwards.com/

Charlie and Marian look forward to seeing you again as they journey together through mystery, murder, and love.

Made in the USA
Columbia, SC
20 May 2020